D0323875

A FRIEND
LIKE THAT

Alfred Slote

A FRIEND LIKE THAT

J. B. LIPPINCOTT   NEW YORK

A Friend Like That
Copyright © 1988 by Alfred Slote
All rights reserved. No part of this book may be
used or reproduced in any manner whatsoever without
written permission except in the case of brief quotations
embodied in critical articles and reviews. Printed in
the United States of America. For information address
J. B. Lippincott Junior Books, 10 East 53rd Street,
New York, N.Y. 10022. Published simultaneously in
Canada by Fitzhenry & Whiteside Limited, Toronto.
1 2 3 4 5 6 7 8 9 10
First Edition

Library of Congress Cataloging-in-Publication Data
Slote, Alfred.
A friend like that / Alfred Slote. — 1st ed.
    p.   cm.
Summary: When eleven-year-old Robby takes drastic steps to stop his widowed
father from developing a new love interest, his friend Beth has to step in and help
him come to terms with the situation.
    ISBN 0-397-32310-7 : $ ISBN 0-397-32311-5 (lib. bdg.) : $
    [1. Remarriage—Fiction.   2. Single-parent family—Fiction.   3. Fathers and sons—
Fiction.   4. Friendship—Fiction.]   I. Title.
PZ7.S635Fr 1988
[Fic]—dc19   87-35053
                                                                        CIP
                                                                        AC

For Barbara St. John

A FRIEND
LIKE THAT

1

I watched Carol shove down with one knee. The suitcase was stuffed.

"You're never gonna make it," I said, wishing it were true.

"I might if you give me a hand, Robby."

"You mean a knee."

"OK," she said, smiling and wiping some beads of sweat from her forehead, "a knee."

I didn't want to give Carol a knee, a hand, not even a little toe. I didn't want to help her leave our house. She was more than a housekeeper. She was a friend.

But I knelt alongside her and placed my right knee alongside her left.

"One, two, three—" she said.

We both pressed downward and the suitcase closed. She snapped the locks.

"Thanks, Robby."

"I wish you'd change your mind."

She laughed. Today was Tuesday. Her wedding to Mr. Lowenfeld was on Sunday. It was a little late to be changing one's mind.

"I'm not stepping out of your life, Robby. We're going to be living in the same town. I'm going to coach your baseball team."

"When's the first practice going to be?"

It was better to talk about baseball than about her leaving.

"As soon as we get back from our honeymoon."

"How long's that gonna be?"

"Only a week."

"A week can make a big difference. All the other teams will be getting a jump on us."

"You can have an informal practice while I'm gone."

"Who starts at shortstop? Me or Beth?"

"Whoever is better."

"I hope you don't show favoritism."

"To which one of you?" she said with a laugh.

"To Beth," I said. Starting Sunday Beth Lowenfeld was going to be Carol's stepdaughter.

Carol looked at me with a faint smile. "I might favor Beth if you don't give me a hand with these boxes."

"What's in them?"

"Books."

"They'll be heavy."

"That's why I need a hand. Especially with this one. Bend your knees when you lift. OK?"

"OK."

"One, two, three . . ."

It was heavy. Books are heavy to read and even heavier to carry. We backed out of her room.

"Where're we taking them?" I grunted.

"Over to the car and then to Art's house," she grunted back.

Art was Mr. Lowenfeld. I called him Mr. Lowenfeld because he'd been my soccer coach. But Carol was Carol. She was an ex-schoolteacher, a graduate student at the university, and our housekeeper. Though that was ending today.

"Easy," she said as we went out the side door and down the cement step onto the driveway and then over to her little yellow VW.

"Are you staying there tonight?"

"No. Just leaving things. I'm staying with my parents till the wedding. Here, let me put my end in first."

We wrestled the big box into the backseat and then walked back to the house.

She tousled my hair. "You know, Robby, when you come to the wedding, you'll be seeing where I grew up."

"I don't want to see where you grew up."

"You'll like it, though. My parents have a backyard almost as big as Tiger Stadium. That's where I learned to play baseball."

"I don't care. I don't see why you have to get married."

Carol laughed. "I don't *have* to. I *want* to. Listen, Robby, how long are you going to keep this up? Peggy was as upset as you and she's fine now."

Peggy's my sister. She's thirteen. I'm eleven. When you're thirteen and a girl, you change your mind quickly about life.

5

"I know," I said, annoyed.

Carol shot me a half-amused look as we went back into the kitchen. There, speak of the devil, was my sister, holding a paper in her hand and looking self-important.

"I've got the seating done, Carol. Do you want to see it?"

"Of course, Peg."

The two of them sat down at the table.

Peg said, "I tried to keep both families together, the way you said, but mix up the singles from both sides. Right?"

"Right. Let's see what it looks like."

The two of them began going over the names of people coming to the wedding. I could see why Carol was doing it, but why Peggy was involved was beyond me.

To start with, Peggy was the one who had originally schemed for *Dad* and Carol to fall in love. You'd think she'd be upset that Mr. Lowenfeld got there first. She didn't seem to be. It was kind of traitorous really.

I knew why Peg was doing it, of course. It was a chance for her to try her hand again at matchmaking. Even though she'd failed the first time with Dad, she liked doing it. She'd fallen in love with matchmaking.

"That's good," Carol said, "putting the Gulden cousins here and the Lowenfeld cousins there. But . . ."

I went back into Carol's room and carried out the

6

rest of her boxes by myself. Once I staggered by them carrying a really heavy box and neither of them so much as looked up.

"I don't really know Art's cousins, Peg," Carol said, "but I saw a picture of Angela once. And she was very pretty."

"I read somewhere that weddings breed weddings," Peggy said.

"Yuck," I said loudly.

They didn't pay attention.

Two days ago when Peg started working on the seating arrangements, she told me she was going to try to put all the single people together. I told her she ought to quit matchmaking for Dad.

"It's bad enough to have to go there and see Carol marry Mr. Lowenfeld without watching you set Dad up with someone else."

"There may be another Carol there, Robby."

"There are no other Carols. You're just having fun. Playing games."

"I'm not just matchmaking for Dad, little brother. I'm also matchmaking for you and me. Dad's ready to remarry, Robby. Some woman's going to grab him. Don't you think we ought to have a say in who our stepmother is going to be?"

That stopped me. Her putting it like that. It *was* a kind of self-protection when you thought about it. A little like fielding a ground ball. You either play the ball or let the ball play you. If you let the ball take charge of you, then you run the chance of a bad bounce and getting hit in your Adam's apple. A bad stepmother could be a lot worse than a smack in your Adam's apple.

But it still seemed wrong to be going to one wedding with another in mind. I wondered what Mom would have thought of it. Mom had died three years ago when we lived in California, but I still know how she'd feel about things.

And I know she wouldn't approve of Peggy matchmaking for Dad.

I loaded Carol's VW till all her boxes were stuffed in. Then I went into the garage and got out my bike. I wasn't going back in and listen to them cluck over who would fall in love with whom at Carol's wedding.

I biked down our pebbly driveway and onto the street, hesitated, and then turned left and headed for Sampson Park. I always go to the park when I feel bad.

It was pretty windy in the park. The only people there were a father showing his little kid how to fly a kite, and way at the far end near the tennis courts I saw a familiar figure banging a ball against the backboard. It was Beth Lowenfeld.

Maybe she'd come to the park for the same reason I had. To get away from wedding plans. Beth was no more happy about her father marrying Carol than I was. For a different reason. She had wanted her parents to remarry, and then after her mom married Mr. Harry Burns, the real estate man she worked for, she decided she didn't want her dad to marry anyone. Period.

I pedaled toward her, my tires bouncing over spongy ground. Till just a couple of weeks ago, there had been a lot of snow in the park. Soon, though, the earth would harden and we could have baseball practice. Honeymoons! Well, we could start without Carol. No one knew how good of a coach she was going to be anyway.

Mr. Lowenfeld had coached the team last year. He couldn't this year and so Carol had volunteered. She had been a varsity softball player in college.

I'd never had a woman coach. Last year I had played shortstop in Watertown, Massachusetts. I could see the guys back in Watertown, especially my best friend, Monk Kelly, giving me the business if a girl beat me out for shortstop in Michigan.

I wished we were moving back to Watertown. It was the best place we'd ever lived. Better even than California, where we had lived before that, and even that was better than Michigan.

As I biked toward the tennis courts, I watched Beth smack the tennis ball. She was a natural athlete. Good in tennis, soccer, hockey, probably baseball too. I'd never seen her play baseball. But this much I know: Not all sports mix well together.

Tennis and baseball, for instance. They don't mix at all. Tennis strokes can ruin your throwing arm. Hit enough serves and overheads and you'll pull those muscles forever.

But I wouldn't tell Beth that. She was my competition for shortstop. More power to her if she wanted to wreck her arm. Carol would put her at second base, where it was only a short throw to first.

I biked past the father teaching his little kid to fly a kite. The kid was sitting on the ground saying: "Can I fly it now?" Dad was having a good time.

Beth was hitting forehands and two-handed backhands. She got down low with each ball and hit it back hard, right around the white line painted on the backboard. That had to be the "net."

I grinned, remembering something Monk Kelly and I had once seen in Watertown. Two little kids were playing tennis without a net and arguing whether a ball one of them hit would have gone over if there was a net. They were really close to fighting too.

"You want to hit some, Robby?"

She'd seen me coming. Probably why she had been hitting so hard. Showing off. It was what I would have done too. She was a competitor.

"No thanks. Hitting a tennis ball can wreck your arm."

The words were out of my mouth before I knew it. How dumb could a guy get?

"Where'd you hear that?"

"Everyone knows that. Some sports just don't work together. Wrong muscles. Tennis and baseball. Swimming and baseball. Some sports go together. Tennis and basketball. They use the same footwork."

"All I asked was if you wanted to hit some."

"I don't have a racket."

"I've got two more at home."

"Which house? Your mom's or your dad's?"

"My mom's. Why?"

" 'Cause Carol's on her way to your dad's house now." That would get to her, I thought.

It did. With a grim little look, she started hitting again.

I grinned. "She's moving in."

"No, she's not. She's just leaving some books and clothes there."

She didn't miss a stroke when answering. She was cool. I wondered if she'd be that cool at shortstop with the other team hollering at her.

Playing sports well is mental as well as physical.

"I guess you're all set for the big wedding."

"Yeah," she said, and hit a sizzling forehand about an inch over the white line.

"Peggy says you're gonna be in the wedding party."

"Uh-huh." She half volleyed with her backhand.

"What're you gonna do?"

"You'll see Sunday." *Thump-thump-thump* went the ball. She didn't miss a beat.

It irritated me.

"I won't see Sunday cause I'm not going."

The words were out of my mouth again before I knew it. But this time her concentration broke. She didn't even swing at the ball coming back. It skipped past her.

"What do you mean you're not going?"

Now I was hung up on my lie.

"I'm not going. That's all."

When you're stuck like that, you better just keep going.

"You have to go. You accepted the invitation."

"I didn't accept. Dad accepted. Weddings aren't for kids. And I don't have to go."

Maybe I didn't have to go at that.

"You do too have to go." She walked after the ball and tapped it up neatly with the head of her racket. Something I've never been able to do.

"Why do *I* have to go to *your* father's wedding?"

"Because it was your fault that they met."

I winced. That hurt a little. Because it was true.

Last August, soon after we arrived in Arborville from Watertown, I had done a dumb thing. Mr. Lowenfeld, who was going to be my soccer coach, had come over to our house to talk to me about it. That was when he and Carol met. Or remet. Since they had known each other as kids back in West Bloomfield but hadn't seen each other for years.

"Well, I didn't bring them together on purpose. So I don't have to go to their wedding. I'm . . . uh, I'm uh . . . gonna be sick on Sunday."

Maybe I *could* be sick.

Beth looked at me scornfully. "With what?"

"Flu. Maybe pneumonia."

She laughed. "See you at the wedding, Robby." She started hitting again.

"No way," I said angrily, and got on my bike and

12

took off. All the way across the park I could hear those irritating *thump-thump-thumps*.

In the middle of the park Dad was still flying his son's kite. And his kid was still watching. Adults run children's lives. That's all there is to it.

I biked out of the park. When I got home, Carol was gone. I was glad. I hoped I never saw her again.

CHAPTER

2

The best time to cut out of a wedding is between the ceremony and the reception.

Right after the judge pronounced Carol and Mr. Lowenfeld husband and wife, I poked Dad in the side.

"How about we go now?"

Dad looked surprised. "Go where?"

"Home. They're married now."

Dad laughed. He doesn't laugh often. He's a pretty serious closed-mouthed guy. But I could always make him laugh. Especially, it seemed, when I wasn't trying.

"There's more to a wedding than a ceremony, Robby. Right now there's a reception line we have to get on."

Reluctantly, I followed Dad and Peg over to the end of a line in Carol's parents' house. You were supposed to shake hands with people. Carol's parents, Mr. Lowenfeld's parents, and Beth Lowenfeld in a white dress and holding a bouquet of roses.

I'd never seen Beth in a dress before. She looked so pretty I almost couldn't look at her.

"I guess you recovered from your sickness," she said.

"Yeah. I did."

I sort of wished Joe Dawkins, Tomzik, Kosmowski, and the other guys on the team could see her like this. Maybe not, though. They might have a hard time accepting her as a ball player if they saw her looking like this.

"That's good," she said.

We stood there awkwardly. "I think we're supposed to shake hands," I said finally.

"We don't have to," she said.

"Good. See you later."

And then I was alongside Carol. "Thanks for coming, Robby," she said, smiling, and gave me a big hug.

I hesitated and then I hugged her back. Though I didn't really want to. I shook hands with Mr. Lowenfeld and then I found Dad and Peg. "*Now* can we go?" I asked.

"Certainly not," Peggy said. "There's a dinner and dancing and the cutting of the cake and the throwing of the bouquet by the bride, and we get to throw rice when the bride and groom leave. Come on. I know where we're sitting."

I bet you do, I thought.

"Here we go, Dad. She's matchmaking."

Dad smiled. "I know, Robby. It's all right. Everybody has a hobby that keeps them out of trouble."

"Yeah, but does it have to be one that gets other people into trouble?"

Peggy was gesturing to us to come to a table that had four people at it with room for three more.

There was an elderly couple, a blond woman, and a boy about Peggy's age.

"How do you do?" said the older woman, smiling. "I'm Martha Slocum and this is my husband, Henry."

"And I'm Angela Nathanson," said the blond woman, flashing a lot of teeth. "I'm a first cousin of Art's, and this is my son Brian."

Brian looked to be about Peg's age or a little older. He had curly dark hair and dark bored eyes. This was a real twofer for Peggy. Someone for Dad and someone for her. I guess the old couple was for me.

The people were waiting for us to introduce ourselves. Dad cleared his throat. He wasn't too good at this sort of thing.

"We're the Millers . . . from Arborville." He laughed, though there was nothing funny that he'd said. "We're friends of Carol and Art. I'm Warren Miller. This is my daughter, Peggy, and my son, Robby."

Mrs. Nathanson clapped her hands. "Aren't you the people Carol was keeping house for when she returned to graduate school?"

"That's right," Dad said with a smile.

"And wasn't Art your soccer coach, Robby? And wasn't that how they met again? Because Art and Carol knew each other as youngsters, you know."

This woman was impossible. She asked questions she knew the answers to. And about stuff I didn't want to be reminded of. She also had more than the normal amount of teeth.

Her son Brian looked at me. "You played on the same soccer team with my cousin Beth?" He made it sound like an insult.

"That's right," I said.

"Was she any good?"

What a snot he was.

"A lot better than me." And probably a lot better than you, I thought.

"Is your son always that modest, Mr. Miller?" Mrs. Nathanson asked. She had at least fifty teeth showing.

"Not modest, just honest," Dad said. "And my name is Warren."

Was Dad falling already for this woman? I couldn't believe it. And where was Mr. Nathanson? I looked to see if Mrs. Nathanson was wearing a wedding ring. She wasn't. Oh, boy, here we go. I shot Peggy a dirty look but she was busy smiling at Brian the Snot.

Two waitresses began putting cups of soup on people's plates.

I took a spoonful.

"Hey, this soup is cold," I said.

"Oh no," Peggy said, rolling her eyes. "We should never take you out in public. It's consommé, and it's supposed to be cold."

She was showing off for Brian.

"Is this the first wedding you've ever gone to?" Brian the Snot asked me.

"No, I average about a wedding a week. Lots of my pals are getting married these days."

"Robby," Peggy said, horrified.

17

Brian the Snot looked amused. "It looks like they get married pretty young in Michigan."

"Actually, we're all older than we look. I'm thirty-five and my sister here is forty-two. It's the Michigan air."

Mrs. Nathanson overheard that and laughed. "Well, that's a good reason to move back to Michigan from California. Since Brian's father and I were divorced last year, I've been thinking about Brian and me returning to Michigan."

She was sending Dad a message. This woman had to be stopped. But fast.

I said, "You know, Mrs. Nathanson, we used to live in California and it's a lot nicer than Michigan." I turned to Brian. "Winters are really cold here. Colder even than Massachusetts, where we lived between California and Michigan. And I'll tell you something else. It's really hard to make friends in Michigan."

"Honestly, Robby," Peggy said. "You didn't have any trouble making friends in Arborville."

"I don't have friends. Just guys I play ball with. I don't have a friend like Monk Kelly back in Watertown.

"What about Beth?" Dad asked. "Isn't she a friend?"

"No," I said. Brian the Snot smiled.

"Robby," Dad said quietly, "a girl can be a friend without being a girlfriend."

"She's just not my friend, Dad." I felt my face getting red.

Luckily for me, a three-musician band began to play just then and Mr. Lowenfeld got up and led

Carol out to the middle of the room. Everyone started looking at them. While that was happening, a hand came in and took away my cold soup. Another hand began putting plates of food on the table. On each plate was a tiny chicken. A dwarf chicken. You could fit it into the small of your hand. I wondered how you were supposed to eat it. With your fingers?

The head table had been served before us. What were they doing about the dwarf chicken? Nothing. They were all watching Carol and Mr. Lowenfeld dance. Beth was staring at them too. I wondered what she was thinking. Could she be thinking about her mother? Wondering what her mom was doing right now. I mean, what do you do on the day your ex-husband gets married? Go picnicking? For that matter, what had Mr. Lowenfeld done on the day Mrs. Lowenfeld had remarried and become Mrs. Burns? Boy, was life ever complicated.

Pretty soon other folks began to dance. Peggy turned to me. "I think you ought to ask Beth to dance, Robby."

"I don't know how to dance."

"Brian," Mrs. Nathanson said, "Beth is your cousin. I think you should ask her to dance."

"Oh, come on, Mother."

"I think it would be nice if one of you two boys asked her to dance," Dad said.

"It ought to be Robby," Peggy said. "He's her friend."

"I just told you, I'm not her friend." I could read my sister like a book. She wanted to dance with Brian the Snot.

"Brian . . ." Mrs. Nathanson looked at him meaningfully.

"Do I have to?"

"Yes," Mrs. Nathanson said.

"Tell you what, Miller," Brian said to me. "I'll flip you for it. Loser asks Beth to dance."

"That's disgusting," Peggy said.

"Boys," Dad said quietly, "I don't think this is very nice."

Even though I hadn't said a thing, Dad had said "boys"—the plural. I knew why. He didn't feel he could correct someone who wasn't his son. So he tried to soften it by lumping us together.

Brian the Snot didn't get the message. "Heads or tails?" he said. He had a quarter in his right hand. "Loser asks her to dance. You call, Miller."

He flipped the coin in the air, caught it with his right hand and slapped it down on his wrist, covering it till I spoke up. I looked toward the head table. Beth was looking at us. She knew exactly what was happening.

I hate seeing people humiliated. "I'll dance with her," I said, and left the table with Brian still holding on to his wrist.

"You wanna dance?"

Something close to anger flickered in Beth's eyes. Then she shrugged. "No."

"Why Beth . . ." Grandma Lowenfeld sitting next to her said, surprised.

Beth's eyes fixed on mine. "Did you lose a bet?"

"No," I said truthfully.

"You and Brian were flipping a coin."

Her grandparents looked shocked.

"He flipped. I didn't. There was no bet."

She didn't believe me. It was getting embarrassing standing there. I felt that everyone in the room was looking at us, knowing I was asking her to dance.

"Let's get out of here," I said. "Let's go outside and throw a ball."

"What ball?"

"I don't know what ball. We could throw your dwarf chicken. It's about the size of a baseball."

Grandpa Lowenfeld laughed. He was all ears. Beth didn't smile. She still thought I'd lost a bet. "Go away," she said.

"Okay," I said. I turned to go, and bumped into a boy my age. He wore a dark suit, white shirt, a red tie. He looked nervous. His nose was quivering as though an invisible fly had landed on it.

"What do you want, Gerald?" Beth practically snapped at him. She was really sore at me but Gerald couldn't know that.

"My mom says I should dance with you."

He couldn't have said anything worse. Beth picked the dwarf chicken off her plate and flung it at him. It hit him smack on his quivering nose.

"Hey," he yelled, "why'd you do that?"

"Because you're stupid, that's why." Beth started looking for another dwarf chicken and that one, I knew, would be meant for me.

I took off.

"What's going on, Beth?" I heard Mr. Lowenfeld say as I went into the main hall.

To the right the hall led to the front door. To the left was the back door. I turned left and stepped out onto a stone terrace. The moment the screen door closed behind me, a big Irish setter came running up. I'm not good with dogs. We never had one. Out of the frying pan and into the fire. I backed up. The dog started leaping on me.

"Easy, man, easy."

I heard the screen door open. Someone coming to my rescue, I hoped.

"His name's Rory," Beth said. The screen door clicked shut behind her.

Rory left me for her. She bent down and let him lick her face.

"Did you get sent outside?"

She nodded.

"How's Gerald doing?"

"He's all right."

"You've got a good arm. Tennis hasn't ruined it yet."

"If I had another one I would have thrown it at you."

"I would've ducked."

"I would've aimed low."

I laughed.

"What's funny?"

"You want to hear a funny story about food throwing? My dad told it to me. It's true, too."

"Sure."

"In a school play once, my dad had to throw a pie in someone's face. From only six feet away. He missed the guy's face and hit him in the neck."

Beth looked up from the dog. "That's funny?"

"What happened next was the funny part. The guy's next line in the play was: 'Why did you throw a pie in my face?' And he said it that way."

"What happened?"

"Dad said: 'I didn't throw it in your face. I threw it in your neck.' "

Beth smiled. "What happened then?"

"Everything fell apart. The next night they gave Dad's part to someone with a better arm. Which is what you get for telling the truth."

"Is that why you tell lies?"

"What're you talking about?"

"You said you didn't ask me to dance because you lost a bet with my cousin Brian."

"I was telling the truth."

She looked at me and then shook her head. "Forget it. It doesn't matter. Brian's a snot."

Amazing. It was my word for him too.

"I was telling the truth, Beth. He wanted to flip but I didn't. I'd like to kill Peggy for putting us at that table."

Beth stroked Rory under his chin. "I told Carol you wouldn't like Brian."

"She didn't do it for me. It was Peggy matchmaking for Dad. You know what I heard her say to Carol?"

"What?"

"Weddings breed weddings. What's that supposed to mean anyway?"

She pulled up Rory's ears and then patted them down. "People go to a wedding and it makes them want to get married." She looked at me. "That's why the bride throws a bouquet to the unmarried women. The one who catches it is supposed to be the next to get married."

"Is Carol gonna throw a bouquet?"

"Yeah."

"Are you gonna try to catch it?"

Beth smiled and shook her head. "I'm too young. So's Peggy."

"Can you be too old to catch it?"

"What do you mean?"

24

"Like your Aunt Angela. She's pretty old to be catching flowers, and besides, she's already been married."

"You're still scared about your dad getting married, aren't you?"

She was talking about what happened last fall, when Peg and I were sure Beth's mom and our dad were going to marry.

The Lowenfelds were the first people we'd met in Michigan. It was Mrs. Lowenfeld who had been responsible for bringing us here. She had received Mr. Lowenfeld's computer software company, Computel, in their divorce settlement and didn't know how to run it. She and Mr. Lowenfeld knew Mom and Dad in California and she traced Dad to Massachusetts, where we were living, and offered him a partnership. He'd run the company because she didn't know anything about computers, and besides, she now had a career selling real estate in Arborville.

Peggy and I were sure Mrs. Lowenfeld wanted to marry Dad. Beth was sure too. And none of us wanted that to happen. Beth because she wanted her folks to get back together again. Peg and me because we just didn't like Mrs. Lowenfeld. And that was when Peg started scheming about Dad and Carol. To block out Mrs. Lowenfeld.

Anyway, nobody's scheme worked. Mrs. Lowenfeld married her boss at the real estate company— Mr. Burns—and Carol was now Mrs. Lowenfeld and Beth's stepmother. Dad was left out in the cold, which suited me fine but not Peggy.

I said, "Sure I'm scared about my dad getting married again. You'd be too if he was your father. He's an engineer. He doesn't know anything about women. And we don't want just anyone for a mother."

"Stepmother."

"OK. Stepmother. It's different in your case. You've got a mother *and* a stepmother. A stepmother would be all we'd have. So she better be a good one. Carol would've been great. But . . ." I shrugged.

It was funny. We'd lived for two years in Watertown, Mass., and none of this marrying stuff had ever come up. Move to Michigan and everyone was getting married or thinking about getting married. As though it was something in the air. Like pollen.

Maybe the answer was to stop breathing.

Rory got tired of being ignored by us. He took off and came back with a red ball and dropped it at Beth's feet.

I grinned. "Hey, Beth, I've seen you throw a midget chicken. Let's see how you do with a ball."

She didn't say anything. She picked up the ball and fired it across the huge lawn. She threw like a guy. A ball player. Rory took off after it.

"You throw like a boy," I said.

"Is that supposed to be a compliment?"

"Yeah."

"Well, it's not. I'm a girl and I can throw as well as you."

Rory dropped the ball in front of her. She picked it up.

"Maybe even better," she said, with a gleam in her

eye. Instead of firing it across the diamond, she shoveled it to me as a shortstop would to a second baseman on the front end of a double play.

I pivoted and fired the ball across the yard. Rory took off after it.

I turned to her. "Don't get any ideas. I'm not a second baseman. I'm gonna challenge you for that shortstop spot all the way."

"You don't scare me," she said with a grin.

The door opened and Carol came outside.

"What are you two doing out here when all the young people are dancing inside?"

"The action's out here," I said, pointing to Rory racing back with the ball in his mouth.

When he saw Carol, he dropped it and ran for her and started jumping up on her bridal gown.

"Rory! Down!" And then Carol gave up and laughed. "All right, boy, all right." She put her face down for him to lick. I wished I had a camera to record that. The bride all in white, her eyes closed, letting a big red dog lick her face.

I stole a look at Beth. Couldn't she see how nice Carol was? But Beth was stony-faced. She just wouldn't admit what a good deal she was getting.

"Rory, bring me the ball," Carol said.

Rory leaped around, pounced on the ball, and dropped it at her feet. He was one smart dog. If he could hit he could probably make our team.

"All right," Carol said, "go get it."

Bridal gown and all, Carol fired the ball across the lawn. It went on a straight line to the farthest edge of the lawn and into the bushes there. Carol threw like a man. . . . I looked at Beth. Like a ball player.

Beth still had no expression on her face. I felt sorry for Carol. It was always gonna be first down and twenty to go through Beth. Carol should have married Dad. She would score touchdowns all the time in our house.

Carol smiled at us. If she was upset by Beth, she didn't show it.

"Listen, you two. The band is playing your kind of music now. All the old folks have sat down."

"I don't know how to dance," I said.

"All you have to do is let your feet listen to the music. Anyone who says he was the best shortstop in Watertown, Massachusetts, ought to be able to do that. Now I want the two of you to get inside before Rory finds the ball and we have to go into extra innings. Let's go!"

We almost made it. Rory found the ball and raced back and caught us at the screen door. He dropped the ball and tried to come in with us.

"No, Rory," Carol said gently, patting him. "Weddings aren't for dogs."

"Or kids," I muttered. Beth nodded.

Carol closed the screen door and looked at us. She knew how we both felt about this wedding. Me wanting her to marry my dad. Beth not wanting her to marry hers.

"Kids, this is a very happy day for me. I so much want it to be a happy one for you too."

There were tears in her eyes.

I suddenly felt ashamed of myself. "I'm happy for you, Carol," I said. It was true. It was just me I wasn't happy for.

Beth didn't say anything. Carol bent down and kissed her on the cheek.

"It will be all right, Beth," she whispered. "I promise you, it will all work out."

Beth broke away and ran into the big room.

"Oh, Robby, how am I going to win her over?"

"She'll be OK. I'll dance with her."

Fred Astaire saves the day.

I went back into the big room. It was just as Carol had said. The music had changed and so had the people dancing. All the young people were dancing now. They were hopping up and down and jerking their arms around.

Beth stood there watching.

"Come on," I said. "Let's dance."

"I don't know how."

"We can do that stuff too."

I went out to the dance floor and began hopping up and down. Peggy and Brian were there jerking their arms this way and that. Not looking at each other. Everyone was jumping around not looking at each other. Half of them had their eyes closed. Elbows were flying.

Beth appeared in front of me and started hopping really good. In time with the music, I mean.

"Hey, all right."

She said, "Look out, Robby."

I got a hard bump from behind. It was Brian the

Snot hopping and jumping and still managing to look bored.

Peggy was in seventh heaven, though. Her eyes were half closed and there was a dreamy smile on her lips. She was hopping in a circle.

I decided to hop in a circle too. It was a mistake, because halfway around, through a screen of moving dancers, I spotted our table. The older couple was gone and Dad was now sitting next to Mrs. Nathanson. I mean like six inches away from her. They were talking to each other as though they were alone on a desert island.

It was like getting hit in the stomach. I almost fell down.

"What's the matter, Robby?" Beth asked.

"Nothing."

I started hopping again.

Dad turned his head toward the dancing. I waved to him. *I'm here too*, I was trying to tell him.

He smiled at me approvingly.

I framed the words "let's go" with my lips and nodded toward the door.

"What are you doing, Robby?" Beth asked.

Dad waved. He wasn't getting the message.

Dad, for Pete's sake . . .

"Robby, are you all right?"

"I'm fine."

I wasn't fine at all. My stomach was all knotted up. I had to get Dad away from that woman.

Someone bumped into me, and then a teenage boy slid between me and Beth, doing jumping jacks. Just like we used to do before junior football back in Watertown.

He slid away still doing jacks.

"Come on, Robby," Beth said, and started doing jumping jacks too.

She was trying to get me back into the dance. Jumping jacks, indeed! I'd like to land on Dad and that woman with a jumping jack.

I jumped and threw my arms out wide. I hit someone. On the side of the head. It was Brian the Snot.

"Watch what you're doing," he snapped.

"Sorry," I said.

The dreamy smile vanished from Peggy's face. She gave me a dirty look. She thought I'd done it on purpose to disrupt them. I hadn't. But . . . What was it our coach in junior football used to say? "Take what the defense gives you. And go with it."

Maybe Peggy had just given me a way to get me and Dad out of here. What did I have to lose?

I turned sideways and timed my next jumping jack to one of Brian's hops. As he went up I went up and flung my arms out wide. I caught Brian off balance. And down he went.

He jumped right up, of course.

"You did that on purpose," he said angrily, and shoved me.

I shoved him back. He was a lot bigger than me. He didn't expect me to shove him back.

Beth was looking at us open-mouthed.

Peggy said, "Stop it, Robby."

Someone said, "Cut it out, guys."

31

Brian shoved me again. "Troublemaker," he said.

I shoved him back again. A girl screamed, and the next thing I knew Carol was pulling us apart. She didn't know Brian but she knew me.

"Robby," she said, "what in God's name are you up to?"

I couldn't meet her eye.

And then Dad took hold of my arm.

"I think it's probably time for us to be leaving, Carol," he said quietly.

Carol didn't say anything. She just looked at me. Off to one side, Mrs. Nathanson and Mr. Lowenfeld were talking to Brian, trying to calm him down. Peggy was almost in tears. The band was still playing but no one was dancing.

I wanted to tell Carol I was sorry. I hadn't meant to disrupt her wedding. I just wanted to break up Dad and that woman.

And I had.

Though from the look on Peggy's face, I knew it was going to be a bad ride home.

CHAPTER

To my surprise, Peg seemed angrier at Dad than at me.

"You gave him just what he wanted. He started that fight on purpose. He knew exactly what he was doing. He wanted us to leave."

I probably should have been quiet. But Dad was defenseless. I'd rather have Peggy sore at me than at Dad anytime.

"The wedding was over, Peg," I said.

"No, it wasn't. We left before the bride and groom."

"Horrors."

She looked daggers at me. "I'm not talking to you anymore."

"Good news for modern man."

I was hoping that would get a laugh out of them, ease things up a bit. "Good news for modern man" had been one of Mom's favorite expressions. It came from the Bible, and she always said it when someone said they were going to take a shower or a bath. Boy, how I wished Mom were here now. She would have understood.

"All right," Dad said. "What's done is done. Let's just try to get home in one piece."

"We missed the cutting of the cake," Peg said, getting started again. "We missed the throwing of the bouquet. We missed the rice."

I knew exactly how her mind worked. When Dad said, "Let's try to get home in one piece," she immediately thought of the piece of wedding cake she had missed because of me. And then everything else.

"I want to know if you're going to let him get away with it. I want to know what you're going to do to him."

Dad looked at her tense face. She was sitting up front with him. I was in the backseat.

"What would you like me to do to him, Peg? Spank him?"

Peggy was silent. She was frustrated. I could feel for her.

"Look," I said, "I'm sorry for what happened."

"No, you're not."

"OK. I'm not. I think your pal Brian is a real snot."

"And you're a clod. A rude, boorish clod. And secondly, that's not why you started that fight. It had nothing to do with Brian."

My stomach did a turn. The last thing I wanted to hear coming out of my sister's mouth was the truth.

Dad saved me. It was as though he *knew* and didn't want to hear it either. "Listen," he said. "It's dark out. I'm not familiar with this road. I want to be able to concentrate so that we don't end up in a ditch. Please, both of you, be quiet for the rest of the way home."

"OK," I said, relieved.

Peggy didn't say anything. But I could feel the hostility pouring out of the back of her neck. I looked out the window. Everything was dark and unfamiliar.

I wished someone would start a song.

We used to go for Sunday drives in California. Coming home it would be dark, and Mom would start singing folk songs like "The Fox Went A-huntin' One Night" or "The Erie Canal." We'd all join in, even Dad, who couldn't sing a lick. It always made the drive home short and fun.

I started thinking about Mom. I'd thought about her during the wedding ceremony. That was when the judge asked Carol and Mr. Lowenfeld would they stick together "till death do you part."

I almost looked at Dad when he said that. I was glad I didn't.

I wished Peggy would start a folk song now. She was sitting in Mom's place in the car. But she didn't.

We drove in silence. Angry silence. And forty minutes later we were home.

Our big, monstrous rented house was dark.

"I wish we had a dog," I said as Dad turned off the motor.

They looked at me, astonished.

"Why do you want a dog, Robby?" Dad asked.

"I don't know. It would be nice to have someone at the door when you come home at night."

I was really just trying to make conversation. Get us back to being a family again.

It was a mistake. Peg said, "Were you planning on going to more weddings, little brother?"

"You never know," I said. It irritated me that she wouldn't get off the subject.

"Well, I know one thing. I'm not going to any more weddings with you."

"Suppose one of your dumb plans succeeds and Dad gets married. Are you not gonna invite me?"

"Oh, shut up," she said.

Which is always an older sister's argument when she knows she's wrong. Dad sighed.

"I don't think Dad is ever going to get married," he said. "No one in her right mind would take on two kids like you. Let's go."

We went in the back door. Carol's room and bathroom were near the back door. She'd been gone since Tuesday, but I still wasn't used to it. It would be Carol's room for a long time.

Dad turned on the inside lights. By the stove clock I saw it was nine-thirty.

"Do you have homework, Peg?" Dad asked.

"I did it yesterday so we could stay to the end of the wedding," she said bitterly.

"Drop it, Peg," Dad warned. "What about you, Robby? Homework?"

I shook my head.

"Do either of you want anything to eat?"

36

"I'd like a piece of wedding cake," Peggy said.

Dad just looked at her. "I'm sorry," Peg said, and ran out of the kitchen. We heard her sobbing as she ran up the stairs.

"There are times," Dad said slowly, "when a mother would come in handy. Do you want some milk?"

"If there're cookies."

"There's a bag of chocolate chips in the bread box."

"Do you want some too?"

"Why not?"

I got the bag of cookies out of the bread box and also got out a plate to put them on. Before Carol arrived to be our housekeeper, we usually just put the bag on the table and reached into it. Carol put stuff on plates; she poured milk into pitchers. The way Mom used to. Well, I'd do that from now on.

"We don't need a mother, Dad. We're fine like we are. You want milk too?"

Dad nodded. "That'd be fine."

For a moment I debated pouring the carton of milk into a pitcher, but that would be laying it on thick. We weren't having dinner or anything. So I poured two glasses and put them on the table next to the cookies, and then I got out two napkins from the drawer. And sat down. Carol couldn't have done it any better.

"Are you gonna look for a new housekeeper, Dad?"

"I'll probably put an ad in the paper."

"You think we can get someone as nice as Carol again?"

"I don't know. Another Carol might be hard to find."

"Mrs. O'Rourke back in Watertown was pretty nice."

I was pushing housekeepers. Housekeepers were better than stepmothers. If they didn't work out, you could always fire them. It's tough to fire a stepmother.

"You still think a lot about Watertown, Robby?"

"All the time." A bit of an exaggeration but basically true.

"What is it exactly that you don't like about Arborville?"

I shrugged. Where to start? "The kids, the schools, the town, the air, the drinking water, the—"

Dad laughed. "Stop. The drinking water's better. The air is cleaner, the schools are better, the teachers are better, the—"

"The principal's scary."

The schools really were better here. And so were the teachers. But our principal at Sampson Park Elementary School had everyone scared of her. Even the parents. Her real name was Miss Bradsbury. But all the kids called her Raspberry.

Dad smiled. "Just behave yourself and you won't be sent to a scary principal. Have another cookie."

I took two more cookies, and for a couple of minutes we sat and drank milk and ate cookies. We didn't talk. Dad's hard to talk to. Maybe I am too . . . for him. But sitting there in our wedding clothes eating cookies . . . it was nice.

Then Dad surprised me. "Did you start that fight, Robby?"

He caught me so quickly, I didn't have time to prepare a story. I nodded. My heart began to pound.

"Was the wedding that awful for you?"

I hesitated. "No," I said truthfully. "It was getting to be kind of fun dancing with Beth."

"Then why did you want to leave?"

I couldn't tell him I wanted us to leave because weddings breed weddings and that I didn't much like Mrs. Nathanson. If he asked me why I didn't like her, I'd probably end up saying something stupid like she had too many teeth. *I'd* end up looking bad, not her.

My best move now would be to shut up and be helpful. I grabbed the empty glasses and plate and put them in the dishwasher.

"The dishwasher's not too full. Should we run it tomorrow?"

Dad just looked at me. I never fooled him. We both knew that. After a moment, he said: "It's late, son. We can talk about it another time." He sounded tired. I felt awful.

"Can you remember to run the dishwasher after breakfast?"

"Sure," I said, relieved. I started to go.

"Robby . . ."

I stopped at the threshold.

"Say good night to Peg. It's no good for a brother and sister to go to sleep not speaking to each other."

"I'll try, but you know how she is."

He smiled tiredly. "Do it anyway."

"OK." I went up the stairs and paused in front of

Peg's door. I could hear her radio playing quietly.

Here goes nothing, I thought.

I knocked quietly, hoping that maybe she was asleep and I wouldn't have to go in but could say "good night" quietly to her closed door.

"Come in, rat," she said.

5

The only light in the room came from the dial of Peggy's clock radio. It cast a soft glow over her face. Her eyes were closed. Her breathing was regular. I hesitated. Maybe I hadn't heard her say "Come in, rat." Maybe I'd just imagined it. Out of sheer guilt.

"You awake?" I asked softly.

Silence. Then: "What do you want?" Her voice was hard.

"I just wanted to say good night."

"Good night."

"I'm sorry about what happened."

"No, you're not."

"I am."

"Did Dad tell you to come up here?"

"Yes."

"OK. You did your duty. Good night."

"Are you gonna hold a grudge forever?"

She opened her eyes and looked at me. "Everyone was having a good time at the wedding except you, so you had to make things miserable for us all."

"You're wrong, Peg. I was having a good time too.

But I didn't like the way you and Carol were setting Dad up for that Mrs. Nathanson. You were pretty upset back in September when you thought Beth's mom wanted to marry Dad, but it's different now that it's Brian's mom, isn't it?"

Beth stared at me like she couldn't believe what I'd said. Then she shook her head. "You are really pitiful. The only reason Carol and I put us at their table is because Dad and Mrs. Nathanson are both single parents."

"Oh? So what about weddings breeding weddings? I heard you say that, you know. Beth told me that's why brides throw bouquets. And guess who Carol might have thrown her bouquet at? And she can throw all right. Believe me, Carol can throw."

"I can't stand it. If you believe in superstitions like that, then there's no talking to you. You're a stupid little boy. Get out of my room."

When they can't argue reasonably with you they insult you. Call you "little." Fact is: I don't believe in superstitions. But that's not the point. The point is other people do.

I looked at Peg. She was angry all over again. I guess I hadn't handled this too well. I decided to make one more attempt to be friendly.

"Do you want me to turn off your radio?"

She didn't deign to answer me.

I reached over. "Leave it on!" she snapped. "And get out of here!"

And then I got angry. "OK. I'm going. But I'll tell you something. If that woman comes to live here as

42

our stepmother and your snotty pal Brian moves in here as my half brother or something, I'm going back to Watertown with or without you and Dad."

She grinned at me. "I won't tell Dad you said that. He might be tempted to call her up and propose on the spot."

"You're really funny."

I slammed the door.

"What was that?" Dad called.

"The wind," I yelled. I went into my room and slammed that door too. "There's a hurricane blowing through the house," I yelled at my closed door.

I turned on the light over my desk and looked at my pictures of Wade Boggs and Larry Bird. I looked at them until I began to calm down. Those guys were my heroes. Boston heroes. I had a picture of Mike Milbury of the Bruins too, but it had got lost in the move. I'd have to go back to Watertown to get another Mike Milbury. Well, I would go back to Watertown to get a picture of Mike. And I'd stay there too. I don't care what Dad says, the schools there aren't that bad.

I turned on my radio and got into my pajamas. I didn't turn off the light yet. I wanted to keep looking at my picture of Bird. Monk Kelly had given it to me. He had cut it out of the *Globe*. It showed Bird running up court, getting back on defense ahead of the other Celtics. It showed his great instincts.

Great instincts made ball players. The only great instinct I had was my ability to get my sister mad at me. You can't score points there.

I turned off the light. Good night, Birdman. Good night, Boggsy. I got school tomorrow.

I closed my eyes. I wasn't sleepy at all. But I knew that the best thing for me to do now was go to sleep. You can't get into trouble when you're sleeping. And sleeping's what I'm really good at. Maybe I could be the Larry Bird of sleeping. If there was an Olympic sleeping team I'd be captain.

My technique for getting to sleep is this: I make up a little scene. Maybe I'm a big-league ball player pitching with bases loaded in front of a hostile crowd, or maybe a government agent capturing a drug runner off the Florida coast. Once in a while I turn myself into an NFL quarterback hopping about under terrific pressure.

Talk about hopping, that dancing had been fun. Peg hadn't believed me when I said that. But it had been.

I thought about Beth. She must be at her mother's by now. Who had taken her home? We could have. Her mother lived just across the park on Hermitage Road. Mr. Lowenfeld had bought a house on Aberdeen Street because that was in the Sampson Park School District too—though not walking distance to the school. Beth could walk to Sampson Park School from her mom's house but she had to take a school bus when she stayed over with her dad. What complicated lives kids lead when their folks divorce.

I thought about Brian the Snot. His folks were divorced too. If they moved back to Michigan he'd never see his dad. That would be terrible, unless his father was a jerk like him.

I grinned in the dark remembering Brian's startled expression when I shoved him back. When you're thirteen and shoving an eleven-year-old, you don't expect to be shoved back. He should have punched me.

I thought about Mrs. Nathanson and her teeth. If she were born an animal, she'd be a shark. Sharks have double sets of teeth. I'd seen that on a *National Geographic Special*.

Wouldn't it be great to be a diver for Jacques Cousteau? I could be swimming underwater investigating an old shipwreck with a camera, maybe an eighteenth-century Spanish galleon loaded with gold, when out of the wreck could come this big white shark grinning at me with all those white teeth.

He'd make a lazy pass at me, looking me over, and then loop back and make another pass, reconnoitering, and then he'd come back all business, aggressive, his mouth open in that devil grin, coming at me fast. I'd swerve coolly and hit him on the snout with the camera as he shot by. I did. And he looked as startled as Brian had. A strange high-pitched sound came out of his mouth. It came again. Loud. Insistent.

I opened my eyes. The doorbell was ringing. I looked at the clock on my radio. Not even eleven. I hadn't been asleep for more than fifteen minutes.

I heard voices outside. I jumped out of bed and went to the window.

45

Standing in the light of our front door was Mrs. Nathanson. I couldn't believe it. Talk about aggressive.

Peggy's window creaked as she slid it up.

"That's very kind of you, Angela," Dad was saying. (Angela already!) "I know they'll be delighted."

Delighted about what?

"I think perhaps you'd better give Peggy hers right away," Mrs. Nathanson said with a laugh. I could almost see those teeth flashing from here. "She'll know why."

"Won't you come in for a cup of coffee?" Dad asked. Was he crazy?

"Thank you. But I've got Beth in the car. I'm taking her back to her mother's house. And Brian's half asleep. It's been a long day for us both."

"You know, I didn't realize that you and Brian were staying in Arborville."

"Well, we didn't know it either, really," she said with a laugh. "But Art kindly said we could use their house till they got back from their honeymoon. I thought it was a good idea because if we do move back to Michigan, Arborville would be a wonderful place to live. And it would be nice for Brian to get a feel for the town while we're here."

A shiver ran through me.

"How long are you staying?" Dad asked. He was only being polite, but a woman like that could mistake politeness for friendliness.

"We're going back Wednesday."

"I hope we can get together before then."

46

"I hope so too."

"It was wonderful meeting you, Warren."

"The same here," Dad said.

She walked to a car in our driveway. I couldn't see Beth or Brian. Dad stood in the pool of light holding something in his hands. He was waiting till she had backed out of our driveway.

When she did, Dad waved. I jumped back into bed. I heard Peggy scurry across the floor and hop into her bed.

The next thing we heard was Dad's footsteps coming up the stairs. He stopped in front of Peggy's door and knocked lightly. No answer.

"She's awake," I said.

"Thanks." He went into her room. I couldn't hear what they were saying, but then he left her room and opened my door.

"Mind if I turn on the light, Robby?"

"No."

He turned on the light, which blinded me for a second.

"That was Mrs. Nathanson—"

"I know. I saw her. What did she want?"

I was letting him know that I didn't think much of her.

Dad ignored my tone. "We left before the cutting of the cake, and she thought we'd like some. It was a very sweet thing to do." He was holding a paper plate with a wedge of yellow wedding cake and a plastic fork on it.

"It would have been a lot better if she had brought

it earlier. Then we wouldn't have had to eat all those cookies."

"I bet you'll find room in your stomach for this."

"You want me to eat it now?"

"You can. Or you can save it till morning. I'll set it down here on your desk. Did you and Peg make up?"

"Sort of."

"What do you mean, sort of?"

"Well, we argued a little. I think I'll go and eat it with her."

"I don't think Peggy's going to eat hers now. You stay right here. Good night, Robby."

"Dad?"

"What?"

"You don't really like her, do you? Mrs. Nathanson?"

"For goodness' sake, son, get her off your mind. She's a nice lady. That's all."

"And the world's full of nice ladies, right?"

"Right." He laughed. "I'll see you in the morning."

It was depressing. He was feeling cheerful again. The visit with that woman had done it.

I waited till he was all the way downstairs. Then I got out of bed and took my wedding cake into Peggy's room. I didn't knock. Her light was out. Her radio was still playing.

"Who's that?"

"Me." I turned on the light.

"Turn off that light."

"I thought we could eat our cake together. And we can't eat in the dark."

"I'm not going to eat my cake now."

"Where is it? I don't even see it."

"It's under my pillow."

"What's it doing there?"

She hesitated. Then she said: "You're supposed to do that for luck."

"What do you mean?"

"Never mind."

"No, what do you mean you're supposed to put your cake under your pillow for luck?"

"Well, you're only supposed to do it if you're a woman. It means you might dream of the man you're going to marry."

"You're putting me on. You just told me a minute ago you didn't believe in superstitions. I bet you ate your whole cake already."

I pulled at her pillow to see. She tried to hold on to it. I yanked it out from under her head and there it was, a crumbling piece of wedding cake. There were crumbs on her sheet already.

"You're not gonna get luck, Peg. You're gonna get roaches."

She lost her temper. I knew right away what was going to happen. When Peg loses her temper she throws things. Mom used to throw stuff too when she got mad. It's in the genes.

Peg started looking around for something to heave at me. The pillow was the logical thing but I had it.

The only other nearby object was her clock radio, but it was plugged into the wall. And that left the cake.

She didn't hesitate. That's how angry she was. She picked up her piece of wedding cake and threw it at me.

Unlike Beth and Carol, thank goodness, Peggy throws like a girl. Meaning she can't throw worth beans, or cake. Her cake missed me by a foot and a half and smacked up against the door, where it broke into a hundred pieces.

And now she was really angry. She shoved her blankets off with her feet and started to get out of bed.

"Here," I said quickly, "dream about anyone you want."

I set my cake down on the foot of her bed. That stopped her.

"But you'll probably get food poisoning if you dream about Brian the Snot."

And then, laughing, I took off before she could throw my cake too. I got back into bed. Cakes under pillows, indeed! Throwing bouquets! I'm not against superstitions. There's a time and place for them. They work in sports: like not talking about a no-hitter when your pitcher is throwing one, or not stepping on the third base line your way out to shortstop. But baseball's a game, not real life.

I started thinking again about shortstop. It was a no-win situation trying to beat out a girl. I mean, if you did, you wouldn't get many Brownie points. And if you didn't . . . Well, you might as well get out of town fast. And out of town they'd laugh at you too. Monk would.

Well, I didn't care. Shortstop was my position back home in Watertown. It would be my position here. A close competition would be tough on Carol. It would also be a good test of her as a coach.

I closed my eyes and tried to imagine Carol coaching us. Hitting the ball around. Barking at us. Even though I'd never had a woman coach, I knew they could be tough. Once, back in Watertown, Mr. Boyle, our coach, hadn't brought a resin bag and it was starting to drizzle. We were playing against a team coached by a woman.

Monk was pitching and the ball was getting away from him. It was wet and slippery. Mr. Boyle called time and went over to their bench and asked the coach if we could borrow her resin bag.

"No way, José," she barked. "Go get your own."

Even though it was one of her players who could have been hit by a wild pitch, that's what she said. Woman coaches could be tough.

Mrs. Nathanson was tough. Beneath those blond hairs and behind those white-toothed smiles, she was one tough cookie. Coming out of her way to bring us three little pieces of cake.

I tried picturing Mrs. Nathanson coaching. It didn't work. But I couldn't really picture Carol coaching either. The best thing would be to have a man who knew a lot about baseball coaching us. Better than that would be to have an ex–major leaguer coaching us. Someone like Wade Boggs. Only he wasn't old enough yet. Heck, in a few years I'd be almost as old as Boggs. I could imagine him and me playing on the same team and him slapping the ball around the infield. I was at third base and wearing a Red Sox uniform.

Before he hit the ball to me, Boggsy asked me my name.

"Robby Miller."

"And a punk like you wants to take my position?"

"No, I'm really a shortstop."

"That's what you say. Let's see you try to take my position."

He hit a screaming line drive at me. And then another one and a third. They came at me like bullets. Hitting the dirt in front of me. I got my body in front of each one and caught all of them.

"OK, Rook, now let's see if you can hit."

Now he was pitching and grinning devilishly at me. It's not fair, I thought, the guy I'm competing with shouldn't be testing me at the plate.

He threw me one wicked curve ball after another. I stayed with each one and hit each one right on the nose. Right field, left field, center field. I could do no wrong. In the field or at the bat.

It was beautiful. I should have fallen asleep a long time ago.

No one wants to wake up to ringing. That was why
I set my clock alarm for music. But I awoke to ringing
anyway.

I opened my eyes and looked at the clock dial. It
was only 7:45. My alarm's always set to 8:00. Now
what was going on?

I pushed the lever to the left to turn it off but it
didn't turn off. It went on ringing. It wasn't my alarm
at all. It was the telephone ringing out in the hall and
in Dad's office and downstairs in the kitchen. The
phone ringing all over the house. Who would call us
at 7:45 A.M.? And why wasn't Dad or Peg answering
it? They were both up. Dad usually left for work
before I left for school, and Peggy usually left for
junior high before Dad left.

I heard the bathroom door open and Peggy rush
into the hall. "Hello," she said, sounding annoyed.

And then her voice changed. To sweetness. "Oh,
no. We're all awake. Except for my brother." Her
voice sounded all quavery, like she'd fallen into a

bowl of jelly. "Thank you so much, Mrs. Nathanson. It was delicious."

Her again! Could you believe it? The day hadn't even started and here she was coming at us again.

"Oh, I'm sure it would be all right. I'll ask my teacher. Yes, Dad's here. . . . He's in the basement putting in a load of wash. No, it's no bother. I'm sure he's done by now. Hang on."

She put the phone down and ran down the stairs. Seconds later I heard the two of them coming up from the basement. Peggy was talking fast. I heard the word "supper." She was briefing him. She wouldn't brief me. I'd have to do my own intelligence work.

I got out of bed and tiptoed over to the phone and lifted it gently, covering the mouthpiece with my hand.

Dad was saying: "I think it's a wonderful idea, Angela, Brian sitting in on classes. It would be a very practical way for him to get a sense of the schools in Arborville."

"To tell you the truth, Warren, it wasn't my idea. Brian said that Peggy suggested it to him at the wedding. He doesn't even know I'm calling you now. But I'm delighted you don't disapprove. I didn't want to seem presumptuous . . . and then calling so early. But when I mentioned the idea to Beth after we drove away from your house last night, she informed me that junior high started at 8:15. Since we're leaving Wednesday, tomorrow would be the only possible day for Brian. And, of course, we'd have to get permission today . . ."

"I'm sure it'll work out," Dad said. "Peggy will speak with her teacher. And as for calling early . . . I've been awake for hours."

"And doing the wash." Mrs. Nathanson laughed. "I'm impressed."

Dad laughed. "I am too."

It was awful. But worse was yet to come.

"Where are you and Brian eating supper tonight?" Dad asked.

"Why . . . I don't know."

"Let me propose something. Carol has left us two large casseroles. It would be impossible for the three of us to finish even one. So why don't you and Brian come over for a true family supper tonight?"

"Oh, but—"

"I insist. I was planning on leaving work early anyway today. Why don't the two of you come over around five and we can show you our house?"

"Are you sure we wouldn't be imposing?"

"Positive."

"Let me bring something for dinner, then. A—"

I felt a hard jab in my back. Peggy was standing there. Her face was furious. "Hang up" . . . she framed the words silently with her lips.

I hung up as softly as I could. "I thought it was for me," I said lamely.

"I *bet* you did. I've a good mind to tell Dad."

"Tell him. I don't care."

I went into the bathroom and shut the door.

"I won't tell him on one condition," Peggy said through the door.

"What's that?"

"On the condition that you don't make a pest of yourself if they have supper with us tonight."

"And that was your idea too, wasn't it?"

"What do you mean, 'too'?"

"Brian going to school with you to see what it's like . . . that also was your brainstorm."

She was silent. A true admission.

"Why don't you quit scheming, Peggy?"

"I'm scheming for Dad's happiness."

"Bull. You're scheming 'cause you've got a crush on Brian the Snot. Well, as far as I'm concerned, the four of you can elope together. I hope you'll all be happy ever after." I flushed the toilet and began washing my hands and face. "I also hope you know what you're getting us into," I said over the noise of the sink. "If we end up with her as our stepmother, then it's all over with our family. Do you think Mom would have liked that woman?"

I scrubbed my face with a washcloth. Mom had taught me to do that.

"Mom never wore lipstick and didn't dye her hair and didn't have a phony laugh and all those teeth. And Mom never schemed the way that woman schemes. Did you ever stop to think what Mom would want for us? Answer me that!"

I opened the door. Peggy couldn't answer me that

because she wasn't there. She was down at the front door saying good-bye to Dad. I felt like a fool.

"Dad, one more thing," she was saying downstairs. "If Mrs. Owens says it's OK for Brian to come to school with me, should I call him at Mr. Lowenfeld's and ask him to meet me there?"

"Let's talk about it at supper tonight. They're going to come at five o'clock. I want you and Robby here then too."

"Oh, Dad, it's so neat. I mean here we were strangers in town just a few months ago, and now we're showing someone else around."

"That's the way it is sometimes." Dad laughed. "You better get going."

Here came Dad's standard joke each morning to us both. "Have a good day at school—and learn something too!"

Peg laughed dutifully. Dad's not a very funny guy, but we love him so much we've learned to laugh at the same bad joke each day.

I got dressed and went downstairs. Dad was getting some cheese out of the refrigerator. He smiled over his shoulder at me. He looked happy.

"Morning, Robby."

I was about to say: "What's so good about it?" but had the sense not to.

"Good morning."

"How'd you sleep?"

"OK."

"There's juice in the fridge. There's Rice Krispies

and Raisin Bran on the counter. I won't be able to get home for lunch today, so I'm going to make you a sandwich to take to school."

"I can make my own sandwich."

"I know you can. But I like doing it. How about cheese, lettuce, and tomato?"

"No tomato."

"Tomato's good for you."

I was about to say: "So why do you ask?" But again I had the sense to keep my mouth shut. Though I really do wonder why parents always ask you what you want and then tell you what you should have. If I live to be a thousand years old I'll never understand that. I just hope I'm not like that when I become a father.

Dad started making my sandwich. He's an engineer but he's not very good with his hands. He's a computer software person, not hardware. I mention this because he was having a hard time right now getting the cheese slices apart. I almost laughed, remembering how it was when he and I and Peggy did the supermarket shopping after Mom died and Dad couldn't get the plastic bags apart. You know the ones I mean? They hang down from rollers in the produce section and after you rip off a sheet you have to separate the ends so you can have a bag. Sometimes it's hard to do. In fact, it got so that Peg, Dad, and I used to have contests to see who could rub their ends open first. Peggy usually won.

Finally, Dad pried two cheese slices apart. "By the

way," he said casually, too casually, "did you hear the phone ring this morning?"

So that's why he insisted on making a sandwich I could have made for myself. He wanted to let me know about the Nathansons coming but didn't dare meet my eye. This way he could concentrate on cheese slices.

"Yeah, I heard the phone."

"It was Mrs. Nathanson. Do you want mayonnaise?"

"Yeah."

"I invited her and Brian to have family supper with us tonight."

"Why did you do that?"

Dad was now concentrating hard on slicing the tomato. "They don't have a place to eat tonight."

"That's right. I heard they closed all the restaurants in Arborville."

He looked at me and almost cut his finger. "What kind of way to talk is that?"

"What kind of thing to do was that? Inviting them here?"

"It was a friendly thing to do."

"It wasn't friendly to me. I don't like her and I don't like him."

"So you indicated yesterday. Well, son, I've got news for you. You shouldn't have to like people to be nice to them." He sliced the sandwich in half and began wrapping it in waxed paper. "Do you want an apple or a pear for dessert?"

"I don't want anything."

"Come on, Robby, don't be a baby."

"A cookie."

"I'll stick in a cookie but you ought to have some fruit too. These apples are delicious."

He didn't wait to see if I wanted a pear. He put the apple in the bag with the sandwich. Then he got out the bag of chocolate chip cookies and put two in and rolled up the top of the bag.

He put the bag on the table near me. "Listen, there's another reason I've asked them to come to supper tonight."

I held my breath. Oh no, I thought. *Weddings breed weddings.* Please don't say it, I prayed. Don't say you want to marry that woman.

"We've been living in this house almost seven months now and we've never entertained as a family."

I breathed again.

"I believe entertaining in one's home is important. Something kids should grow up accustomed to. One day you and Peggy will be married, have homes, families . . . you should know how to do these things. If your mother were here we'd be entertaining. When Carol was here it didn't occur to us; we were really just getting to know her. Now it seems to me that you and I and Peggy can do it. We're ready for this now."

He had it all justified in his head. He was inviting Mrs. Nathanson over for our sake. God, it makes me mad how people as smart as Dad can fool themselves.

I kept silent, though. I knew that any objection I

raised would only make things worse. Make him more stubborn.

"They'll be here at five. I want you home by five, Robby."

"I'll try."

"Don't try. Be here. I've got to run now. Remember to lock up when you leave."

"I will."

"And run the dishwasher, too."

"OK."

He tousled my head and smiled down at me. "Look here, nobody's going to get married without a lot of warning and talking over among the three of us."

I almost said: "You mean I get a choice there too? Like with the tomato and the apple?" But once again I had the sense to keep my mouth shut. There's a time to mouth off and a time to be quiet. Now was the time to be quiet.

Besides, Dad was getting ready for the second go-round of his daily morning joke.

"Have a good day at school, Robby, and . . ."

Learn something, I thought dismally.

But he fooled me.

". . . be nice to your teacher," he said.

I was so startled that I laughed. A new joke. "I'll give it my best shot," I said.

And that turned out to be a joke too.

7

The usual early-morning soccer game was going on in front of the school when I got there. My best friend in Michigan, Joe Dawkins, was in it. I got on his side. From our baseball team, Billy Littlefield, the center fielder, was in the game—on the other side—and Beth was playing goalie for the other side.

It was a big game. About thirty kids, and pretty raggle-taggle. You could switch sides and no one would notice.

A loose ball came my way. I pounced on it and headed up the right sideline. Joe yelled from the other sideline. He wanted a pass. But nobody ever passed in playground soccer. You kept it till someone took it away from you. And much as I liked Joe, that's what I was going to do.

I galloped past a couple of fourth graders, and then Littlefield and a kid named Mike, who was in the other fifth-grade class, loomed up in front of me. Behind them was Beth, covering the short side of the goal.

There was no way I'd pass to Joe now, but I could fake a pass.

I stopped suddenly and faked kicking to him. I fooled the Mike kid but not Littlefield. He waited for my next move, his feet apart. I kicked it between his legs and then the two of us raced for the ball.

Out of the corner of my eye, I saw Beth leaving the goal mouth to try to beat me to the ball. I saw her but Littlefield, her teammate, didn't. We were both on a collision course with her. Beth was leaning forward as she ran, getting set to scoop it up. She'd be completely unprotected. Running head down like that.

I did the only thing possible. Just a few feet from where he would have slammed into Beth, I shoved Billy Littlefield with my elbow, hard as I could, almost exactly the way I'd shoved Brian at the wedding yesterday.

And Billy went down just the way Brian had. I veered off and let Beth scoop up the ball and kick it downfield.

And then I got mad at her.

"Are you nuts? You can get really hurt playing with your head down."

"You don't have to look after me," she snapped, and ran back to the goal. The bell rang. No one paid attention to it. The game flowed on.

"You can get hurt too, Miller," Littlefield said, coming up to me. His hands were doubled up into fists. "What's the big idea?"

"I had to do that, Billy. You would have run into her."

"Oh. So now you're looking after the other team's goalie?"

"For Pete's sake, Billy."

"Or maybe you're in love with Beth Lowenfeld."

I almost punched him. I should have. It would have solved a lot of problems for me, but I didn't know that then.

A whistle blew. It was our teacher, Mrs. Janssen. She was standing on the front steps of the school.

"The bell has rung. Everyone line up," she called.

The little kids were on line already. They always are. Fifth and sixth graders are too cool to get on line. We sort of straggle in. The girls too.

Littlefield and I were still standing toe to toe, though, glaring at each other. Joe Dawkins came over fast. He sized up the situation immediately and grinned at us both.

"That was a great move, Robby," he said. "Real NFL cornerback stuff."

"This isn't football, Joe," Littlefield snapped, "it's soccer."

"Come on, Billy," Joe said. "You would have really hurt Beth. And she's our shortstop. We got to keep her in good health. We don't want Robby getting her position just 'cause she's injured."

It was high-level peacemaking. Littlefield un-tensed a little.

"She shouldn't play with guys if she can't look after herself," he grumbled.

64

"She can," I said. "In fact, she's sore at me now."

Joe laughed. "I wouldn't get into a punch-out with Beth Lowenfeld, Robby."

I laughed too. "I'll try not to."

Littlefield wasn't laughing. The line moved quickly into the school. We walked slowly toward the front door. Joe stayed between me and Littlefield.

"If you three are not inside the building in ten seconds, you can report to Miss Bradsbury's office," Mrs. Janssen called to us.

"Big threat," Joe said.

"I don't know about that," Littlefield said, moving a little faster. "You remember when I got into a fight with Simonds last year in front of his locker?"

"Yeah," Joe said.

"I got sent to Raspberry's office and she kept me there two hours."

"Two hours?" we said.

"Yeah. It's automatic. If you're caught fighting she sends for your parents. Both my folks work and neither one could come till five. So Raspberry kept me there till five."

"That's a long time to be with Raspberry," Joe said.

"Tell me about it," Littlefield said.

It hit me then. Just like that. Bingo. Just the way it dawned on me at the wedding how I could get us out of there by bopping Brian. It dawned on me now how I could wreck Dad's big plans for today. I'd had the perfect opportunity a couple of minutes ago with Littlefield, but I didn't know then about Raspberry's rules.

Now I had to count on Joe to understand.

"Joe," I said, "I need to have a fight with you right now."

Joe looked at me, surprised. "What for?"

"There's no time to explain." I grabbed him around the neck and started wrestling him down.

"Quit fooling," Joe said, laughing. He escaped from my grasp and ran for the front door.

Billy started to run too. I grabbed his arm.

Mrs. Janssen blew her whistle at us.

"You two—" she began.

I didn't wait for her to finish her sentence. I jumped on Billy and wrestled him to the ground.

As we went down I caught a glimpse of Joe standing wide-eyed on the front steps of the school.

And that was all I saw because by then Mrs. Janssen had arrived and was yanking me to my feet.

"You, young man, are headed straight for Miss Bradsbury's office," she said.

"Yes, ma'am." I said cheerfully, and ran to the front door.

"You're crazy," Joe said to me.

"Like a fox," I laughed. "See you later."

I took the steps two at a time and made a beeline for Raspberry's office.

I wasn't the only kid there. A second grader with a nosebleed was sitting in the outer office. The school secretary, Mrs. Carlson, was holding a handkerchief to his nose.

"There, it's getting better already, isn't it, Todd?" she was saying.

"No," Todd said.

Mrs. Carlson looked up at me. "What can I do for you, young man?"

"I've been sent to the principal's office," I said, doing my best to look worried.

"Oh . . . by whom?"

"Mrs. Janssen. For fighting."

"I see. Well, just sit down. I'm sure Mrs. Janssen will be along in a minute. I'll tell Miss Bradsbury you're here. Now, can you hold that handkerchief to your nose, Todd?"

The kid nodded. Mrs. Carlson went into the inner office. I took a seat opposite the second grader.

"Someone hit you?" I asked.

"Terry Casey."

"You hit him back?"

"She's a girl."

"That's OK. You hit her back?"

He shook his head. "I don't like to fight."

"No one does. But sometimes you have to."

Mrs. Janssen came into the office and gave me a severe look.

"Well, you got here fast enough."

I didn't say anything. There's nothing to say to that.

"Before we go in to see Miss Bradsbury, do you mind telling me what that was all about?"

"I got into a fight with Littlefield."

"I know that. I'm asking why."

I thought hard. "He almost ran over Beth in the game."

"That's it?" She seemed surprised.

"Yes, ma'am."

Mrs. Carlson came out. "Hello, Mrs. Janssen . . ."

Don't you love how teachers and school clerks always call each other Mr. and Mrs. when kids are around, but when they're in the teachers' lounge it's Mary or Anne . . . except for Raspberry. They always call her Miss Bradsbury. Everyone calls her Miss Bradsbury. I bet Raspberry's mother called her that when she was born.

"Miss Bradsbury will see him now," Mrs. Carlson said. "How's the nosebleed coming, Todd?"

"It's still bleeding," Todd said cheerfully. I guess he didn't like his class much.

Mrs. Janssen held the door open and I went in first. Raspberry was standing next to the window. I want to say right off that she didn't look tough or mean. Which was what made her doubly dangerous. Raspberry was kind of pretty.

She had short brown hair, wore tailored suits, and always had a cool smile on her lips. Though you never felt that she was smiling inside. You felt that inside, she was made of silicon chips that were measuring you and filing you away for future punishment.

The other thing when you stood in front of her: you got the feeling you were only one of a thousand kids who'd stood before her in this very office and she'd heard every excuse imaginable.

"Miss Bradsbury, I asked Robby to come here because he was fighting with Billy Littlefield."

"I know, Mrs. Janssen," Raspberry said, looking at me with those cool blue eyes, "I saw it all out the window. He and Billy were walking along and the next second Robby jumped on him."

"Billy claims he'd done nothing to provoke him. Not only that, he said Robby had wanted to fight with Joe Dawkins just before that."

Not quite accurate, I thought. I wanted to *have* a fight with Joe, not fight with him. There's a big difference.

"Is that true, Robby?" Raspberry asked me.

"Is what true?"

"That you wanted to fight with Joe Dawkins before that?"

"No, ma'am," I said.

"Thank you, Mrs. Janssen," Raspberry said crisply. "I'll send Robby along in a few minutes." She turned to me and pointed to a low-slung brown leather chair. "Sit down, please."

I sat down and down and down and down. Almost out of sight. There'd be no quick escape from a chair like this. It was no accident a principal like Raspberry kept a chair like this for her victims.

She didn't sit. She stood in front of her desk looking down at me.

"Suppose you tell me what's going on, Robby." Her voice sounded kind.

This is when she's most dangerous, I thought.

"It was about the soccer game. He was playing unfairly."

"Why didn't your fight take place during the game, then? Why did you wait till you were walking to the door?"

It would be nice to tell her the truth: that I hadn't known fighting was an automatic ticket to her office and I could get my dad to come here at five o'clock, and not be home for *her.*

But of course you don't tell the truth to someone like Raspberry. They'd clobber you. I didn't say anything. I just sat there looking stupid.

For some reason she didn't push it. She studied me as though I were a strange fish that had just washed up on a beach.

In the outer office I could hear Mrs. Carlson telling Todd that his nose had stopped bleeding and he could go back to his class now. I could also hear the sounds of other classes . . . laughter.

If I wasn't in a jam, it would have been nice just sitting here listening to the sounds of the school.

"Robby . . ." she said softly.

"Yes, ma'am."

"By any chance, did you *want* to get into trouble this morning?"

I was stunned. How had she known that? It had to be a shot in the dark. She wasn't a mind reader. Or was she?

Maybe I'd better stop thinking. Give her a blank face. Start thinking about nothing. I tried to do just that. Which isn't so easy. Thinking blank. I thought about a blank wall I knew back in Watertown. It was an old factory I used to walk by on my way to school.

"Were you *trying* to get sent to my office, Robby?"

I concentrated on the blank brick wall in Watertown. Someone had written on it: *Patti and Joe, '42.* Monk told me that was the class of 1942 from the high school. That's how old that wall was. You don't see walls that old in Michigan.

"You're not answering my question, Robby."

"No, ma'am."

She looked at me for a moment. "Are things all right at home?"

I breathed out slowly. This woman got more dangerous every second. "They're fine," I said.

"You live with your father, don't you?"

"And my sister."

"Your sister goes to junior high, doesn't she?"

I nodded. I was surprised she knew that.

"Your father is a widower, isn't he?"

"Yes." She'd done her homework on me all right. Could she know this much about every kid in the school?

"Joe Dawkins is a good friend of yours, isn't he?"

I nodded.

"Billy Littlefield is also on your baseball team, isn't he?"

"Yes, ma'am."

"Suddenly you want to fight with both of them."

She paused . . . waiting for me to pick up on it. I didn't.

She studied me some more and then out of nowhere she smiled. "Robby, why don't we just leave it that you got up on the wrong side of the bed this morning. You can go back to class now."

I was dumbstruck. I stared at her. "What?"

"I said, you can go back to class now."

"But . . . but aren't you going to keep me after school? Aren't you going to send for my father?"

I blurted it out and knew immediately it was a mistake. She smiled.

"No, I'm afraid you're going to have to find another way to accomplish that. You could get hurt the way you're going about it now. You may return to class, Robby."

I was dismissed. Just like that. And she was laughing at me. I hated her. I hated her for being so smart. And I hated her for not following her own rules.

She opened the door for me to leave.

I marched past her angrily. Past Mrs. Carlson, who looked surprised to see me come out so soon. I marched down the hall to my classroom. I could hear Mrs. Janssen talking about the French explorers in America. When I came into the room, she stopped. She looked at me. Everyone else looked at me. I avoided their eyes and went to my seat and sat there and looked at the desk. The same stupid brown desk with someone's initials, P.K., carved in it.

Mrs. Janssen did me a big favor by not calling on me. After a while I took out our big *Explorations* reader, but I didn't pay much attention. I should never have come to class. I should've kept going out the door.

After that unit, we did some science—winds and how they work—and then a social studies unit on immigration in the United States. Mrs. Janssen said that after recess we'd put the two units together: explorers and immigration. I usually looked forward to recess, but I kind of dreaded it now . . . seeing everyone, having to explain myself.

As I was going down the stairs, some kids asked me if I was going to be kept after school in Raspberry's office. When I told them no, they said I was pretty lucky. Real lucky, I thought bitterly.

I hung back. I didn't want to face Joe, Littlefield, any of the guys . . . even Beth.

Finally, Mrs. Janssen came down the stairs.

"Aren't you going outside?" she asked me.

I nodded. And went out. Another soccer game was going on.

"Robby."

I turned around. It was Beth. She was waiting for me.

"I don't want to talk about it," I said.

"What're you so mad at?"

"I'm mad at this school, this town. If I could, I'd get on the first bus going to Massachusetts."

"Why did you want to fight with Joe?"

"I told you, I don't want to talk about it."

"He's sore. So's Littlefield."

"I'm worried, really worried."

"They're coming over here."

I looked toward the flagpole. Where the guys always met. Joe, Littlefield, Tomzik from Fischer's class,

Kosmowski, Winkelman, were all walking this way. They looked like a sheriff's posse.

"You better take off," I said to Beth.

She shook her head. She didn't look like she did at the wedding yesterday. She looked like a tomboy again.

The guys came and stood around me in a circle. I could tell there was going to be a fight. Me, and who with I didn't know yet. I could see Mrs. Janssen looking this way a little concerned. I didn't need her help. I didn't need anyone's help.

Joe said, "We wanna know what's going on, Robby."

"Nothing's going on," I said.

"Bull," he said. "First you wanna have a fight with me and then you hit Littlefield. And when I ask you if you're crazy, you say 'like a fox.' "

Joe was my best friend in Arborville . . . not as good a friend as Monk Kelly back in Watertown, but my best friend here. And he looked at me as though I was his sworn enemy.

"Forget it," I said. "It had nothing to do with you guys."

Littlefield took a deep breath. "I'm not scared of you, Miller. I'm willing to fight you anytime, right now included."

A lot of kids started coming around then. Kids always gather around when they see a fight is going to start. Like vultures spotting a kill.

"I don't want to fight you or anyone," I said.

"Miller's yellow," someone said.

"No, he's not," Beth said.

74

"You keep out of it, Beth," Joe said.

"Don't tell me what to do, Joe Dawkins," Beth said.

I turned to her. "He's right, it's—" That was as far as I got. Littlefield blindsided me. He hit me when I wasn't even looking at him. It stung but it didn't hurt. Not really.

"Look, Billy," I began, "I don't want to—"

He hit me again, and then in self-protection I had to grab his arms. We wrestled each other to the ground.

Everyone except Beth was yelling: "Get him, Billy."

It was all so stupid and senseless. My heart wasn't in fighting Littlefield or anyone. We rolled around in the dirt, him pummeling me.

"Robby's not even fighting back," Tomzik said.

"He's a coward," Joe said.

"Get off of him, Billy," Beth said.

She began pulling at Littlefield, who was trying to get me into a headlock. I jerked my head, and then all of a sudden I was free. It wasn't Beth who'd freed me. It was Mrs. Janssen. She had yanked Littlefield up to his feet.

She was furious. "All right, both of you into the building immediately!"

Her hands propelling us forward, she marched us up the steps. Littlefield was protesting loudly. "I was just getting even. He hit me this morning."

"You can explain it to Miss Bradsbury," Mrs. Janssen said angrily. "I've had enough of both of you."

You plan things and nothing works. Don't plan and everything succeeds.

"So," Miss Bradsbury said, and she didn't look surprised. In fact, she looked amused again. "Back again. And *you* made the principal's office too this time, Billy. Congratulations to you both. Well, Billy, shall we start with you?"

She was seated behind her desk. We were standing in front of it. I had dirt all over my face and hair. My shirt was dirty. Littlefield was messed up too.

"Robby started it, Miss Bradsbury. He jumped me this morning."

"And so you were just getting even, is that it?"

"Yes, ma'am."

"You were here just a week ago for fighting, weren't you, Billy?" Her voice was gentle and ominous.

Billy swallowed. "Yes, but . . . this wasn't my fault. He wanted to fight with Joe too this morning."

"I heard about that. All right, Billy. I want you to go back to class right now and stay there. You can forget about recess."

Billy looked at her as though he couldn't believe it. "Aren't you gonna send for my folks?"

"I may. It depends on your behavior for the rest of today. Is that clear?"

"Yes, ma'am." Billy shot me a look of triumph as he left the room. When the door closed behind him, Miss Bradsbury turned those cool, amused, blue eyes on me.

"You win, Robby. Now I shall ask your father to come to school."

I did my best to look sad. But my tongue betrayed me: "He's at work. Computel. Do you want his phone number?"

"I have it in your school file, thanks."

Seconds later, I heard the phone get answered at Dad's company: "Computel. Can I help you?"

This is Janet Bradsbury, principal of Sampson Park School. I'd like to speak with Mr. Miller, please."

There was no "Can I ask what this is about?" stuff. Dad had told the receptionist at Computel to put through immediately all calls concerning his kids.

Miss Bradsbury's long, slender fingers tapped on her desk. I wondered if her fingers always did that when she was calling up a parent. She must have called over ten thousand parents in her lifetime.

"Hello. This is Warren Miller . . ." I heard Dad say. Miss Bradsbury sat back in her chair, swiveled, and from then on I couldn't quite hear Dad's end of the conversation. I could hear his voice but not his words.

I could hear Miss Bradsbury, though. Clear and crisp. Like a machine gun. "This is Janet Bradsbury from Sampson Park School, Mr. Miller. Your son Robby is in my office right now. No, he's quite all right. But he's been in fights twice today, and our school policy is to send for a parent when there's any fighting at all." Pause. "With a classmate."

Pause. Dad's voice again.

"I don't quite know what about, Mr. Miller," she said. "I thought your presence might help us get to the bottom of the problem."

Dad said something. Miss Bradsbury frowned.

"I appreciate your willingness to come right away, but my policy is that these visits take place *after* school. We don't want students missing any more work than they already have—"

Dad's voice.

"I see, but—" she said.

Dad's voice again. I was amazed. He was arguing with her. Dad, who hardly ever argued with anyone. Dad, who was usually so mild.

Miss Bradsbury looked annoyed. "I see. Well, if that's the case, then you'll just have to come now."

Oh, no, I thought.

"He'll be in my office. Good-bye."

She hung up.

"It seems you have dinner guests tonight and your father has to be home early."

That's just the point, I wanted to say to her. That's what the fights are all about.

There was a long silence between us. I could hear classroom noises floating down the hall again . . . and

two kids walking in the hall, probably to the bathroom.

"Robby, do you not like it here in Arborville?"

I shook my head. Not meeting her eye. She'd be
inside my head before I knew it.

"Yet, for someone who's relatively new to town,
it seems to me you've made a good transition. You
were on a soccer team in the fall, a hockey team in
winter, and you're on a baseball team this spring. I
get the feeling you're quite popular. I know you're a
friend of Beth Lowenfeld's."

"Her mother and my dad own a business together."

"I understand her father just got remarried."

"Yesterday. We went to the wedding."

"Was it nice?"

I looked at her. Now what was she after? What did
she care about the wedding yesterday?

"It was boring. Except when an Irish setter chased
a ball."

She smiled. "I take it, then, it was held in someone's house?"

"Yeah. Carol's."

"I love home weddings. Who's Carol?" she asked,
almost as an afterthought.

"She was our housekeeper when we first got here."

"So you have to get a new housekeeper now, don't
you?" She was on the trail all right. I felt like saying:
"You're getting warm, now cold . . . colder . . ."

I nodded. Yes, we had to get a new housekeeper
now.

"Who's doing the cooking at the moment?"

"Dad. And Peggy. We're all right. We could even get by without a housekeeper."

The moment I said "even," I knew it was a mistake.

She smiled. "Not to mention . . ." She paused, waiting for me to fill in the gap. I didn't. I saw how she operated. Sort of half said things and waited for you to fill in the rest of the sentence. Miss Bradsbury would have made a great district attorney. Which was what principals were anyway.

She sighed. "Well, at least, then, it's understandable why your father wants to be home early for the dinner party."

"He's not gonna have to cook. Just warm up casseroles."

She laughed. "Well, maybe he's planning a special dessert."

"She's bringing dessert."

Mistake number two.

"Who's she?" she asked casually.

"No one," I said. I clenched my fists. I was through talking.

"Why don't you tell me what's going on, Robby? Perhaps I could help."

I shook my head. For the first time I felt trapped in that deep leather chair. In a TV show, at least, I could send for a defense lawyer.

"Robby, I've been a principal in this school for ten years, and you're the first pupil I've met who wanted and worked—and I should add was willing to suffer—to have his father come to my office."

"I don't want him to come now," I muttered.

"I see."

No, you don't.

"You wanted him to come *after* school, is that it?"

Yes, you do.

Her next question came out of left field. It had nothing to do with anything. And she had no right to ask it.

"When did your mother die, Robby?"

I stared at her. Then I said bitterly: "You know everything else about me. My soccer team and my hockey team and my friends. Don't you have in your file when my mom died?"

"No," she said.

"Three years ago. I was eight."

"Was she nice?"

"She was wonderful."

"Tell me about your mom."

"I can't." And then I started to cry. Trapped in Miss Bradsbury's big leather chair, I burst into tears and before I knew it I was telling her everything. Everything that had *nothing* to do with my mother. Everything about the wedding and Peggy maneuvering to get the Nathansons here and their coming here at five o'clock and why I wanted Dad here at school at five o'clock. It all sounded so stupid and babyish that I hated myself as I ran my mouth but I told it anyway. And, of all people, to Miss Bradsbury, I mean Raspberry, the meanest principal in Arborville.

When I was done I couldn't look at her. And you know what she said?

"Why don't you go to the bathroom and wash up?"

It was the kind of thing Mom would have said. And that almost made me cry some more.

I stood up. "Miss Bradsbury . . ."

"Yes, Robby?"

"Would you not tell my father all that?"

She thought about it for a moment. "On one condition," she said.

I waited.

"That you tell him yourself."

I shook my head. "I couldn't do that."

"Why not?"

"I just couldn't."

"Well," she said with her cool smile, "if you don't, I will. It's as simple as that. You know, Robby, ninety-nine percent of the time pain and heartache come from not being able to talk with people we love and who love us. You and your father have to learn to talk to each other openly and frankly. So I want you to tell your father everything you just told me. I'll excuse myself when he arrives. Any questions?"

"No."

"Good. Now go and wash up and come right back."

She was tough and smart. I was glad to get out of there.

In the outer office, Mrs. Carlson was putting papers into a folder. She smiled at me. I went across the hall into the boys' bathroom. I took my time. In the mirror I examined my smeary, teary, dirty face. My shirt was dirty too.

"Good going, Robby," I said to my image. "You've

really done it now. Made a complete ass of yourself. Cried in the principal's office. Made enemies of your friends and taken Dad away from his work in the middle of the day. You touched all bases and you were out at every one."

The door opened. And that same little second grader who'd had the bloody nose came into the bathroom. He looked around. Wondering who I was talking to.

I started to wash my face.

"Hi," he said.

I ignored him.

"I don't wash my face afterward," the kid said.

I looked at him. Was he being funny?

"I don't even wash my hands," he said.

There was a knock on the door.

"Are you still in there, Robby?" It was Mrs. Carlson.

I wiped off with a paper towel. "Yes, ma'am."

"Your father's here," she said.

"I'll be right out." I got another towel and blew my nose in it. Then I examined myself in the mirror some more. My eyes were still red. The little second grader watched me curiously.

"Are you in trouble?" he asked.

"Yeah," I said.

"Me too."

"Terry Casey still after you?"

He nodded.

"That means she probably likes you."

He shook his head. "She wouldn't hit me if she liked me." You could see he'd thought about it.

"Well, just keep away from her."

"She hits me during recess."

"Can't you keep away from her during recess?"

"No."

"Then don't go out for recess. Go to the bathroom."

"That's what I'm doing," he said.

I laughed. The kid was sharp. And I was a great one to be giving advice.

I opened the door. "Well, good luck anyway, Todd."

"How do you know my name?"

"I heard Mrs. Carlson talking to you."

"Oh."

The door swung shut. Mrs. Carlson, on her way down the hall, the folder in her hand, called to me: "Go right in. Your father's there now."

I didn't have to go into Miss Bradsbury's office to hear Dad's voice. It was unnaturally loud. I stood outside and listened through the door.

"Look, Mrs. Bradsbury—"

"*Miss* Bradsbury," she said.

"Sorry. *Miss* Bradsbury."

It was almost funny. Dad, who's usually patient and mild, was having a hard time being either. Now he knew what it was like to be called to the principal's office.

"Can we talk sensibly about this, Miss Bradsbury? You call me away from my job in the middle of the day—"

"On the contrary, Mr. Miller, I asked you to come at the end of the day. It was you who insisted on coming right away. Even though you knew this would make Robby miss classwork."

She was too quick for Dad.

"I'm not available at the end of the day," Dad said, through gritted teeth.

"Evidently."

Poor Pop.

"Can we talk about Robby?"

"Of course. That *is* the purpose of your coming here."

I could picture Dad gritting his teeth again. Trying to stay engineer calm.

"Look here. Robby is not a fighting boy. We came here from New England, where the public schools aren't as good as they are here, and Robby never got into trouble there once. He's a good kid."

"He's a wonderful kid," Miss Bradsbury said, which really surprised me. I didn't think she liked me at all.

"Then why on earth does he get into two, not one, but two fights today?"

"I think you ought to ask him precisely that, Mr. Miller."

"I intend to. I'm just very curious why you won't tell me."

"As I told you a moment ago, Mr. Miller, I promised Robby that you would hear it from his own lips."

"It's that bad?" Dad said.

"Perhaps. Perhaps not. It is something for the two of you to talk about. I gather you and Robby don't communicate easily."

"Nonsense," Dad said.

Mrs. Carlson came back into the outer office. She looked surprised to see me. "Haven't you gone in yet?" she asked.

I shook my head.

She gave me a you-should-be-ashamed-of-yourself

look. She knew I had been eavesdropping. She knocked on Miss Bradsbury's door.

"Yes?"

"Robby's here."

"Please send him in, Mrs. Carlson."

I went in. Dad was sitting in the deep chair, looking as trapped as I had.

"Thank you, Mrs. Carlson," Miss Bradsbury said. She looked at me carefully and I knew she was wondering where I had been all this time. "Please sit down, Robby."

There was a straight chair at the other end of the desk. I had to cross in front of Dad to get to it. He held out his hand, blocking me. He peered up at my face.

"You all right?"

"Yeah."

He let me go. I sat down.

"Do you want to tell me what this is all about, son?"

I hesitated. I glanced across the desk at Miss Bradsbury.

She smiled. "I believe I have some work to do with Mrs. Carlson. Call me if you need me."

She closed the door firmly . . . meaningfully.

Dad shook his head. "Impossible woman," he said. He turned to me. "Well, what's going on?"

"It's hard to explain . . ."

He waited.

"Could we talk about it at home?"

"Robby, I didn't leave work in order to talk about

it at home. There won't be time at home. The Nathansons are coming at five. . . . If you could explain it to her, you certainly ought to be able to explain it to me."

That sounded reasonable enough. I took a deep breath. "Well . . ." I began . . . and then stopped. I couldn't do it. I simply couldn't do it. I couldn't tell my own father what I had just told a stranger.

He looked at me, wondering what the matter was. I'd have to tell him something. I took a deep breath. "This guy and I, Dad, we had a couple of fights . . ." I hesitated.

"I already know that, Robby. What were you fighting about?"

"Soccer. He was going to cream Beth. She was in goal. She was going for the ball. So was he. The funny part was they were on the same side. I was on the other side. But he would have knocked her down, so I knocked him down first. Later, he got mad and we had a second fight."

"That's it?"

"Yeah."

"Are you sure that's all there was to it?"

"Yes."

"What's so hard to explain about that?"

I shrugged.

Dad shook his head. "I don't see why she couldn't have told me that. And why I had to be called here for that."

"They do it automatically."

"Are you all right now?"

"Sure." I felt guilty about lying. I was making Miss Bradsbury look bad, but she'd never know. I was getting out of it all right.

"Robby, in the two years we lived in New England, I was never called to school once because of you."

"I'd give anything to go back there."

"When you're grown up you can live wherever you want. Till then, we're living in Michigan." He made it sound like a life sentence.

Dad stood up. "No more nonsense, son, all right?"

I nodded.

"And remember to be home by five at the latest. Peggy's coming home right after school to make snacks."

The junior high ends at 3:00. We end at 3:30.

Dad opened the door. Miss Bradsbury and Mrs. Carlson were looking at some papers on Mrs. Carlson's desk. Miss Bradsbury looked up.

"We're done," Dad said. And then to my horror he said: "Robby has explained everything to me, Miss Bradsbury. And while I certainly don't approve of his fighting, I do approve of his defending Beth Lowenfeld."

Miss Bradsbury's eyes widened. So did Mrs. Carlson's. Dad plunged right on.

"I am curious about one thing, Miss Bradsbury. Did you also send for the parents of the boy who started the fight with Robby?"

Silence. "I see," Miss Bradsbury said. She looked thoughtful. "I think perhaps the three of us ought to talk together."

"I don't think there's anything more to talk about," Dad said. "I'm satisfied with Robby's account of what happened."

"I'm sure you are, Mr. Miller. I'm just not sure we each heard the same account."

"Can I be excused?" I said.

"I don't think so, Robby," Miss Bradsbury said.

"I have to go to the bathroom."

I had learned something from Todd, the little second grader. When trouble thickens, go to the bathroom.

Before she could stop me I walked out of the office. She came after me.

"One second, Robby."

I stopped. I turned to face her but I couldn't meet her eye. "I'm sorry," I said. "I . . . couldn't tell him."

She was silent a moment. "All right," she said. "I can understand that. But I think it may be best that your father and I talk alone."

That would be horrible too. Maybe even worse. How could I face Dad after that? I looked down the corridor. The school noises were all there . . . echoing. Laughter, voices, a piano playing . . .

She wasn't angry with me. Her voice was gentle. "The world's not going to come to an end, Robby, if you tell him or I tell him. You have to trust your father's love for you."

She put her hand under my chin and tilted my head up so that our eyes did meet.

"Be brave," she said.

I nodded.

She smiled. "You don't really have to go to the bathroom, do you?"

I shook my head.

"Go back to class, then."

I turned and walked fast down the hall. I knew she was watching me. I turned the corner and stopped. She couldn't see me now.

As I stood there I heard laughter erupt from the other fifth-grade class; Mrs. Fischer's voice floated out telling the kids to open their readers; I heard shouts and cries from the gym. The school was like a living animal. An animal that could eat you up alive.

I couldn't just stand here. I walked down the hall past the art room with its familiar paste smells, the same smells of kindergarten too, any school's first smells. I walked past a noisy fourth-grade classroom, past the library where two sixth-grade girls were lying on a rug reading. I paused in front of our class's lockers, which were opposite our room. I could hear Mrs. Janssen's voice.

"All right, Tammy . . ." She was talking to Tammy Weiss, who was a smart kid. "You tell the class how the three nations differed in their approach to the new world."

"Well," Tammy said, "the French didn't stay because they were only interested in furs, and the Spanish were only interested in gold, but the English settlers who were fleeing persecution wanted to start a new life somewhere else. So they stayed."

"Excellent, Tammy. They wanted to make a new

start . . . a *new* England, from which we get the term New England. John, could you tell us what the result of this was for our future nation?"

I could see Littlefield and Beth. They sat up front a couple of seats apart. Joe sat in back. I couldn't see him.

"Robby's out in the hall, Mrs. Janssen," someone said.

I was spotted.

Beth and Littlefield looked at me. And then some other kids left their desks to look at me, as though I were some kind of freak. Mrs. Janssen came to the door. "Are you coming to class, Robby?"

"I got to get something from my locker," I said. I turned my back to her and fiddled with my "com." I hadn't the slightest idea what I was going to do after I got my locker open. I couldn't go back to Miss Bradsbury's office, where she was spilling the beans to Dad. I didn't see how I could ever face Dad again. I didn't want to go into our room, where Joe Dawkins, my best friend in Arborville, had become an enemy. Where Billy Littlefield sat gloating. And where Beth sat there probably feeling sorry for me. That might be the worst thing of all: Beth Lowenfeld feeling sorry for me.

What I'd really like to do was go somewhere like the English colonists and make a new life for myself.

"Did Miss Bradsbury send you back to class, Robby?" Mrs. Janssen was speaking to me.

I didn't answer. I kept fiddling with my lock until I got it open. I heard her then tell the class—they must have been all standing in the doorway watching

The Robby Miller Combination Lock Show—I heard her tell them to go back to their seats.

I got my locker open and grabbed the only thing inside it—my lunch. I shut the locker and locked the lock.

When I turned around, she had her back to me and was addressing the class.

"I'm going to talk with Robby for a moment. While I'm gone, I want you to consider what is happening in the world today that might remind you of the English colonists fleeing persecution.

"Think about people wanting to leave Central America, Vietnam, Russia. . . . One reason we study history, children, is not only to find out what was going on in the past but to see what lessons can be learned for today. The past is a guide to the present. Think about that. . . ."

I thought about that. Fast and hard I thought about that. And suddenly I knew what I was going to do.

"Robby," Mrs. Janssen shouted.

I ran down the hall, past a second-grade classroom, past the stairs to the gym, past the music room, and then out the exit door and down the stairs that lead to the parking lot.

If the English colonists could run away, so could I. Especially since we were both going to the same place.

"Can I help you, sonny?" The ticket agent had a mean face. He looked as though he never smiled.

"I'd like to buy a ticket to . . . uh, Boston."

I was going to say Watertown, but no bus would go from Arborville, Michigan, to Watertown, Massachusetts. I'd go to Boston and then take the T (the Boston subway) out to Watertown.

"Boston, eh?" He opened a big book and began turning pages, licking his index finger as he turned each page. "Running away from home, are you?"

I blinked. I couldn't believe he said that. But he wasn't even looking at me. He was still turning pages. It was probably his idea of a joke. Something he said to every kid who came in to buy a bus ticket. He was the kind of adult who got his kicks teasing kids.

"I'm buying this ticket for someone else." My voice sounded calmer than I felt.

"That's what they all say," he said. "Let's see, Arborville . . . Boston. Be ninety-five dollars one way. One hundred and fifty-nine round trip."

I stared a him. "That much?"

"I don't set the prices, sonny. If I did, I wouldn't be workin' here. Next bus leaves at one o'clock, changes at Cleveland and Buffalo."

He closed the book.

"Ninety-five dollars . . ." I shook my head. That was a lot. I had it, but it was a lot.

I pulled two big old sweat socks full of change and dollar bills out of my hockey bag.

He leaned over the counter to see what I was doing.

I emptied one sock out on his counter. An avalanche of coins started rolling toward him. He looked alarmed. I pulled the dollar bills and the five-dollar bills out with my fingers.

"Now listen here. You stop this right now." He blocked the flow of coins with his stomach. "You can't do this."

"It's good money," I said.

"Maybe, but this ain't no bank. I don't have time to count all this, and phew . . . get those socks out of jhere."

They were unwashed socks, but they didn't smell that bad. "Here's dollar bills and five-dollar bills," I said. "I'll help you count the coins."

I started separating pennies from nickels and nickels from dimes and dimes from quarters. The ticket agent looked disgusted.

"Look here, sonny, does your mother know you're here?"

I made a big pile of quarters and started another one. "My mom's dead."

"Oh. Uh . . . well, does your father know?"

"Sure," I lied. And then a second lie followed. "I'm buying this ticket for my cousin. Here's at least fifty quarters in these two piles. I got lots more quarters and dimes."

"All right," he grumped. "I'll do the countin'. You're just blame lucky I ain't busy now."

I looked around. The only other people in the bus station were a tall, tired-looking woman with two little girls. The girls looked like twins. One was sucking her thumb and holding a beat-up doll. The other was trying to escape from her mother's grasp.

"Settle down, Ticia," the mother said quietly.

"Ten dollars," the grumpy ticket agent said, and made a pencil note. He put the quarters in a drawer and started counting again.

"Banks got machines that do this," he snapped.

"I didn't have time to go to the bank."

He made another pile of quarters. "How come your cousin don't buy his own ticket?"

"He's too busy."

"Well, it's a good thing he don't want a round-trip ticket."

You don't have to worry about that, I thought.

"If a customer comes in, I'm gonna stop this nonsense and wait on him."

"Yes, sir."

He was dying for a customer to come in, but none did. Finally, he was done. He shoved the rest of the coins back toward me. "Keep the change," he said, making a poor joke.

I scooped up the rest of the money and put it into my other sock. I put the sock back in my bag.

"Can you tell me when the bus gets to Boston?"

"Soon as I get through putting this money away." He didn't have room in his regular change drawer.

"Your cousin know the bus leaves in a half hour?"

"Sure," I said.

"OK," he said. He punched some buttons and gave me a long ticket that said Arborville-Boston.

"Now what was that you was wantin' to know?"

"When do I get to Boston?"

He leaned forward. His eyes got suspicious. "I thought you said you was buying this for your cousin."

I winced. "I am," I said.

"Y'are runnin' away, ain't ya? Now look here, son, this ain't none of my business but . . . how old are you anyway?"

"Thirteen."

"You don't look thirteen. You look more like nine."

"I'm eleven," I said angrily.

"Ha! Fooled you, didn't I? Didn't think you looked no thirteen. I got a grandson thirteen what looks thirteen."

I didn't say anything. I wanted to get the arrival time in Boston, so I could call Monk.

"Let me tell you, sonny, it ain't no easy trip. You got to change buses in Cleveland and then again at Buffalo, and I don't know what happens at Albany. That's in New York State. Long ways from here." He

97

grinned wolfishly. "Change your mind about going?"

I tried to give him a cool smile, a Miss Bradsbury kind of smile. I don't think he even noticed it.

"The reason I'm asking about the time is 'cause I'm supposed to call my grandma and let her know what time my cousin is getting in."

He sneered at me. "Still holdin' on to that cousin. . . . Well, it's your funeral." Shaking his head as though he really cared, he opened up the thick book and licked his index finger again and started turning pages.

I looked around. The mother was still holding on to the wriggly twin.

"You're old enough to know how to sit still, Ticia," the mother said.

Ticia shook her head. "I wanna run around, Ma."

"Six thirty A.M.," the ticket agent said. "That's when you'll get there. When all the bums'll be wakin' up in Boston bus terminal. I hope your grandma won't mind that."

"She won't. She likes bums."

The only grandma I knew well was Dad's ma. Grandma Margaret. I was pretty sure she didn't like bums. She had lived on Army bases all her life with Grampa Frank, and they don't have many bums on army bases.

I checked the clock. It was twelve thirty-five. I had about twenty-five minutes. *If* the bus was on time.

"Is there a phone here?"

I had almost made the mistake of calling Monk

from home. But it hit me that they could trace that call and I didn't want anyone coming after me.

The sourpuss agent made one last attempt to trap me. He squinted at me. "You know the area code in Boston?"

"617," I said promptly.

"There's a phone out on the sidewalk," he said reluctantly.

As I walked out, Ticia, the wriggly one, tried to join me. The mother quietly yanked her back.

Up close I saw Ticia and her sister couldn't be more than five years old. I was sure glad I wasn't traveling with them.

The phone booth was on the corner of Huron and Ashley. Traffic was moving fast down Huron Street, which is one of the main streets out of Arborville.

I dialed Monk's number.

The operator came on the line and said to deposit one dollar and ninety-five cents for the first minute. This was when it was good to have piggy-bank change. I had that much in my pocket. But putting all that money in the coin slots took time. In fact, I thought the bus could come while I was depositing nickels, dimes, and quarters, but finally the operator said "Thank you," and I heard the phone ringing in Monk's house.

I was excited. I'd only talked to Monk once since we moved. To invite him out to see a college football game. Monk said, before we left, that he'd go to Michigan for that OK. We used to watch their football games on TV. But he couldn't come. Still, it was wonderful just talking to him.

"Hello," a high-pitched woman's voice said.

It was Mrs. Kelly, a large, jolly woman who had always had a thin band of sweat above her upper lip. She had tiny laughing eyes.

"Mrs. Kelly, this is Robby Miller."

"Robby!" She squealed in delight. Behind me the traffic roared by.

"Where are you, child?"

"In Michigan. Can I come visit you?"

"Of course you can. When?"

"Now."

"Now? What about school?"

"It's spring vacation here." Lying to the ticket agent helped. Your first lie is always your hardest. After that, the others just fit right in as though they were truths.

"Is Monk . . . I mean, is John there?"

Monk's real name was John, but no one except his mom called him that. Monk got his name because from the time he could walk he could also climb. "Climb anything," his dad said. "Trees, flagpoles, street signs. You name it, he'd climb it. I called him a monkey right off." From then on, Monk's name was "Monk."

Once when Monk was complaining about his nickname, I told him it could've been worse. "Heck, you coulda been called ape."

Monk laughed. He never took anything seriously.

And he always stood up for you. He was loyal. Not like the kids around here.

"John's not here now, Robby," his mom said. "He's in school. We don't have spring break here till next week."

I don't know why I figured Monk would be on spring vacation. Maybe because Brian the Snot was and I thought everyone who lived out of town might be.

"But you can visit anyway, Robby. We'd all love to see you. How's your fahthah?" Which was how they pronounced "father" around Boston.

"He's fine."

"And how's his business doin'?"

"Great."

"That's nice. Now exactly when did you plan on coming?"

"In about a half hour."

"What?"

I laughed. "I won't be there in a half hour but the bus is leaving in a half hour."

"A bus? Robby, that'll take you forever."

"That's OK. It'll be fun. It goes to Cleveland and Buffalo and Albany."

"Won't your fahthah let you fly?"

"Uh . . . he . . . says the bus is safer."

"But you'll be up all night on it."

"That's OK."

"Well, it wouldn't be OK with me. What time does it get to Boston?"

Here goes nothing, I thought. "Six thirty in the morning."

"Oh, my goodness, child. Are you sure you want to do this?"

"Yeah."

"All right. John and I'll go down on the T and meet you. You can come back with us. School don't start till nine, so you two can have breakfast together and I'll make sure you get a long nap while he's in school." Mrs. Kelly had always felt sorry for me because my mom had died. She sort of tried to be a second mother to me.

"I can't get over this. You comin' here. Now, you give my love to your fahthah and we'll see you in the mornin'. Now, you're sure you're comin'?"

"Positive."

"If you don't, you call us."

"I will."

"And be careful on that bus. Some crazy people ride buses these days. Don't get off it and wander away. Do you have enough money?"

"Plenty."

"Do you have something to eat? They don't always stop when you're hungry."

"I've got a sandwich."

"One sandwich?"

"And two cookies and an apple."

"Robby, that's not enough. Is your fahthah there?"

"I'm calling from the bus station."

"Somehow this doesn't feel right to me."

"I'll be fine, Mrs. Kelly. Tell Monk I'm coming. Good-bye, Mrs. Kelly."

I hung up. What a swell lady. The phone rang again.

"Please deposit ninety cents for additional time," the operator said.

I dug out more money and deposited it.

"Thank you," the operator said.

"Where are you going, Robby?" another voice said. Behind me.

That second voice was just about the last voice I expected to hear in downtown Arborville in the middle of the day. I looked past her.

"Don't worry. I'm alone," Beth Lowenfeld said.

11

"How'd you get here, Beth?"

"The same way you did. Walked."

"Don't be funny. You're supposed to be in school right now."

"So're you."

Traffic came roaring down Huron Street after the light changed. I kept one eye on the corner of Huron and Main. The bus should be coming from that direction.

"How'd you even know I was here?"

"You said this morning you wanted to take a bus to Watertown. I just put two and two together."

She was smarter than my dad and Miss Bradsbury put together.

"Who knows you're here?"

"No one. Is that where you're going? Watertown?"

"Never mind where I'm going. It's none of your business where I'm going."

It was a relief to know she hadn't told anyone where she was going. And she wouldn't lie about that. Unlike some other kids I know, Beth Lowenfeld didn't tell lies.

"Listen," I said, and grinned, "it's nice of you to come down and see me off, but you're gonna get in trouble leaving school."

She shook her head. "It's lunch hour. I was supposed to go home for lunch."

"Then your mom's gonna be worried."

"She's not there. She and Harry are having an open house. I was supposed to make my own lunch today."

"Then you're gonna get hungry. Take this sandwich and go back to school."

I got out the cheese and tomato sandwich Dad had made me, and handed it to her. She didn't take it.

"Don't run away from home, Robby."

"I'm not running away *from* home. I'm *going* home. I know what running away is. I did that once."

I had too. When I was all of five years old. Back in California. I'd had a fight with Mom. I had left one of my toys on the kitchen floor and she came in the kitchen and tripped over it. It was a Sherman tank model that Grampa Miller had given me. Grampa had commanded a tank company in World War II. It was my favorite toy.

Mom got furious.

"I hate this," she said through gritted teeth. She picked up the little tank and threw it against the wall. It broke. The driver's head rolled across the kitchen floor and under the stove.

"I'm sick and tired of your not picking up your toys."

I stared at the broken pieces.

"There are rules for living in this family, Robby Miller. And if you want to go on living here, you've got to obey them. And the first rule is to pick up your toys."

I got the driver's head out from under the stove and picked up all the broken parts.

"I don't want to live here anymore," I said.

"Then leave."

I carried the pieces of the tank to my room and put them in my backpack. Then I went to the bathroom and got my toothbrush. I put that in the backpack too. Then I slung the pack over my shoulders and went to the front door. Mom was watching me from the kitchen.

"Where do you think you're going?"

"You said I should leave."

"I didn't say you *should* leave. I just told you we had certain rules in this house, and if you didn't obey them, then you could leave."

"I can't obey them," I said.

"Then you better go," she said.

"I am."

"Good-bye," she said.

"Good-bye," I said.

Mom and I were a couple of hardheads, all right. I went out the front door. It was about seven o'clock and dark. November. It wasn't cold the way Massachusetts and Michigan get in November, but there was a sharp dry wind blowing. I didn't even have a sweater on. Or one packed.

106

I walked down our driveway. I looked back. Mom was watching me from the front door.

"Good-bye," I said.

"Good-bye," she said.

I kept going till I was out of sight, on the other side of the hedge that separated our house from the people next door. Then I sat down under the hedge. I was cold. I ought to have gone back for a sweater. But I couldn't. Not with her waiting for me to come back. I didn't know what to do. Or where to go.

I don't know how long I sat there shivering below the hedge, but after a while I saw Dad's car come down our street. We lived on a dead end, a little circle. His headlights swept over me. I didn't duck.

A moment later I heard the garage door open and he drove in. Soon after that, Mom came out of the house and around the hedge right to where I was sitting. She had a bag in her hand and a sweater.

"You're not properly dressed for running away, Robby. Here's a sweater and a cheese sandwich for when you get hungry."

"Thanks," I said, and burst into tears. Mom grabbed me and she started crying too. We cried and hugged each other. Oh, how we hugged each other.

"I don't want to run away," I cried.

"I don't want you to run away," she cried.

Dad came out and looked at us both. He shook his head. "How would you two chips off the same stubborn block like to come in and have a hot chocolate?"

I nodded through my tears. So did Mom.

The next day I had a new Army tank. It wasn't as good as Grampa's. I started picking up my toys.

It's funny how a memory like that comes back to you. Beth was looking at me curiously. Wondering where I'd gone. I couldn't tell her.

Out of the bus station came the tall mother and her twin daughters. The mother was still holding on to Ticia. They were looking toward the corner of Main and Huron.

The agent must have announced the bus's arrival.

"Do you have money?" Beth asked me.

"Why? You want to give me some?"

"I have twelve dollars."

"What're you going to school with twelve dollars for?"

"Lunch money."

"Lunch money? What are they serving? Steak? Besides, you said you went home for lunch."

"Only when I'm staying with my mom. When I come from my dad's house, I eat lunch in school. I usually forget to bring money and Dad forgets too, so Mom gave me twelve dollars to pay what I owe."

"Carol'll remember stuff like that. Listen, you be nice to Carol. She's a swell person."

A big gray-and-blue interstate bus turned the corner and headed toward us.

"Something else, Beth," I said quickly. "You tell Carol I'm sorry I can't play for her, 'cause I know she's gonna be a great coach."

"Tell her yourself," Beth said.

The bus said CLEVELAND.

"Are you going to Cleveland?" Beth asked, as though it was the North Pole.

I grinned. "What's wrong with Cleveland?"

The bus stopped about fifteen feet past us. I thrust my lunch into Beth's hands. "Eat it and be quiet," I said, and headed for the door. She ran with me.

"Why are you going to Cleveland?"

" 'Cause it's a great town. The Indians, the Browns, the Cavs. I got friends in Cleveland." Which was a big fat lie, of course.

"You've got friends here too, Robby." She tugged at my elbow.

"I *had* friends here."

"I'm your friend," Beth said.

"Listen, I'm talking about a friend like Monk Kelly. He's getting up tomorrow morning at five thirty to go to Boston and meet me at the bus station. I call that a real friend."

"So you *are* going to Watertown," she said.

Why did I talk so much?

The driver was the first one out. He went over to the luggage compartment in the bottom of the bus and pulled up on the lever. The metal door rolled up. Three people waited for him to haul out their suitcases.

"I know why you're leaving," Beth said desperately. "You're scared of Billy Littlefield."

I laughed. "Nice try, but I could beat up Littlefield with one hand tied behind my back."

"You'd never beat me out for shortstop," she said. "Carol even said that."

"Carol'd never say something like that. And when the day comes that I couldn't beat you out for shortstop . . . heck, let's quit talking."

"Robby . . ." She was trying to block me from entering the bus.

"This is the 990 for Cleveland, with a stop in Toledo. Tickets, please," the driver called out.

"Ticia, come back," the mother said.

As the mother had opened her pocketbook to give the driver their tickets, Ticia the Wriggly had broken away and was squatting in front of the luggage compartment, turning her head sideways to see what was inside.

"I want to see inside the bus's belly, Mom."

"Now you've seen," the mother said wearily, and took her by the hand.

"I didn't see," Ticia said.

The mother hauled Ticia back to the bus.

I laughed. "This is why buses are fun to travel. Well, so long, Beth. It's been nice knowing you." I brushed by her.

I hate long good-byes.

I gave the driver my ticket and went up into the bus and walked to the back.

I sat down on the seat cushion and looked out. Beth was gone. The driver was going into the terminal—I guess to make sure he had all his passengers. The mother and her daughters were seated in the middle of the bus. The mother was seated with

110

Ticia. The other twin sat across the aisle from Ticia.

Sure enough, Ticia the Wriggly got out of her seat and walked back to where I was sitting and stared at me the way little kids will.

"Hi," I said.

"Hi," she said, and turned and ran back down the aisle. Her mother looked at her and shook her head. "Don't you ever get tired?"

"No," Ticia said, but sat down.

The driver got back in and was about to close the doors when a Last-Minute Louie rapped on them.

The driver opened the doors. Someone thrust a ticket at him. He looked at it. "Toledo. First stop."

The passenger stepped up into the bus. It was Beth.

12

She took a seat in front of me.

"Are you crazy? Where do you think you're going?"

"To Toledo," she said, without turning around.

"What're you gonna do in Toledo?"

"I don't know. I've never been there."

"Get off this bus right now, Beth," I ordered.

But it was too late. We were moving. We'd circle the block and then head up Huron, and then up Washtenaw, past the university women's athletic fields, past the big fraternity and sorority houses with their huge lawns, and then out of town past gas stations, car washes, strip malls, fast-food restaurants, drive-in banks . . . till we came to a big green highway sign that said: U.S. 23, Toledo.

I got up and told Beth to move over. She did and I sat down beside her.

"Why're you doing this to me? What did I ever do to you?"

She looked at me. "What am I doing to you?"

"Putting pressure on me to go back. But I'm not

going back. I'm going to Watertown, and I don't care where you get off."

"You want half your sandwich?"

"No! How much did your ticket to Toledo cost?"

"Eleven dollars."

"That leaves you one dollar. How are you gonna get home?"

She shook her head.

"Your mother's gonna be worried out of her mind."

"I told you, she's having an open house."

Beth's mom was in the real estate business day and night with her new husband, Harry F. Burns.

"I'm gonna ask the driver to let you off at the corner of Washtenaw and South U. We'll probably stop for a light there. You can walk home from there."

She looked at me. "Will you get off?"

"No."

"I won't either, then."

"I've got nothing to do with you," I yelled at her. Ticia turned around and looked at us. Her mother was sleeping.

"You're scaring that little girl, Robby," Beth said.

"Nothing can scare her. Listen to me, Beth—"

"Do you want half a sandwich?"

"No," I yelled again. Ticia came down the aisle and stared at us.

"You fighting?" she asked Beth.

Beth shook her head.

The mother, eyes still closed, groped around instinctively for Ticia. Her hands met emptiness. She opened her eyes.

"Ticia, come back here."

"You were fighting," Ticia said.

The mother took Ticia the Wriggly by the arm. "Excuse us," she said softly to Beth and me, and led Ticia back to their seat. This time she made Ticia sit on the inside. She'd have a hard time escaping again.

"If I ever become a parent, I hope I don't have a daughter," I said.

Beth smiled. "There's an apple in here and two cookies."

"I'm not hungry."

We were coming to the corner of South U and Washtenaw. It was a big intersection. I would shout to the driver once we were stopped. I looked ahead. The light turned green ahead of us and there were no cars waiting. We shot through the intersection and shot our last chance to stop before Toledo.

On the sidewalks university students were hurrying to campus.

"I'll split the apple with you," she said.

"I told you I wasn't hungry."

She held out a cookie.

I shook my head. "You're worse than my sister about taking no for an answer. She's always bossing me around too. But at least she's thirteen. You're my age. I'm really sorry for the guy who marries you. Is he ever gonna have problems!"

"You think so?"

"I know so. Look, are you going to call your mother from Toledo to come get you?"

"I told you—" she began.

"Your mom can't be reached."

"And neither can your dad," she added. "He and Raspberry left the school together."

"I know."

Beth was astonished. "How do you know that?"

This was a little embarrassing. "I was in the house when they came by. I went home from school to get clothes and money. In fact, if it wasn't for the money, he and Miss Bradsbury would have found me."

"What do you mean?"

"I had to get money from my piggy banks."

"You mean you paid for your bus ticket to Boston with money from a piggy bank?"

I felt myself blushing. "Two piggy banks. Big ones. You have to break them to get the money out. The first thing I did when I got home was take them down to Dad's workbench in the basement and get a hammer. That was when the front door opened upstairs. I turned off the light.

"Dad shouted: 'Robby, Robby.'

"He must have shouted five times. I felt lousy about not answering, Beth. I love Dad. I love him more than anyone else on earth. And I know he loves me, but I'd made such a mess of everything. I can't even explain it to you. I couldn't explain it to him. And now Miss Bradsbury had told him. I couldn't face him."

"What did you do?"

"You mean in the house? I didn't do anything. I hid in the basement."

"I mean, what did you do that was so awful?"

I shook my head. "You want to hear about the money and how it saved me? Yes or no?"

"OK."

"I heard footsteps going up the stairs. And Dad shouted my name more times. I heard doors opening and closing. I mean, I even think he was looking in closets for me. It was awful. And if he had decided to check the basement, it would have been all over. But he didn't.

" 'He's not here,' I heard him say, and that was when I realized he wasn't alone.

" 'We'll look for him in the park, then,' Miss Bradsbury said."

Beth interrupted my tale. "How come you don't call her Raspberry anymore?"

I stared at her. "Don't I?"

"No, you're calling her Miss Bradsbury all the time."

"Raspberry . . . Bradsbury . . . what's the difference? The big thing was I couldn't believe she was looking for me too.

" 'What makes you think he's in the park?' I heard Dad ask her.

" 'When children are unhappy, Mr. Miller, they always go to places where they were last happy. I've seen Robby playing ball in the park. He was happy there.'

" 'Apparently you know a lot about children,' Dad said. He was being sarcastic, which isn't like him at all.

" 'I've had several thousand children through the years,' she said.

"Dad didn't say anything. She floored him. I could tell that just by listening.

" 'You know, you don't have to get involved in this, Miss Bradsbury,' Dad said.

" 'Nonsense, Mr. Miller. Robby is as much my responsibility as yours. More so during school hours. . . .'

"And that was all I heard. They were gone. Out the front door. If it hadn't been such a close call, I would have laughed out loud. Dad was sure getting a good dose of her. But there was no time for chuckles. If they were going to check out all the places I had been happy in Arborville, they'd be back in a hurry.

"I broke the piggy banks and put the money in two socks that I fished out of a wash basket. Then I went upstairs, put the socks and some clothes in my old Watertown hockey bag and put on my old Watertown warm-up jacket, 'cause there would never be a better time to wear it than now. Then I took off down side streets for the bus station, and you found me."

Our bus was rolling past the junky part of Washtenaw Avenue now. The gas stations and muffler shops and fast-food places. Lots of signs.

Beth said, "Don't you feel bad about your father driving around looking for you right now? Worrying about you?"

"No, I don't. 'Cause he's not really worried about me. If he was, he'd stop trying to marry someone and let the three of us stick together. In fact, I'm glad he's looking for me, because he's stuck with Miss Bradsbury and it serves him right."

I laughed. Beth didn't. "I think you're mean," she said.

"Hey, I didn't ask you to come on this bus. If you don't like it . . ." I was going to say "get off," but she couldn't get off before Toledo.

"Listen, Beth, you didn't do me any favor coming along like this. I'm gonna have to leave you in Toledo. Do you know what city bus stations are like? They're full of weird characters. Bums. Thieves. People sleep in bus stations."

"You can't scare me, Robby."

"I'm not trying to." I was lying. "Even if I did buy you a ticket back to Arborville, it'd probably be hours before there'd be a bus going back to Arborville. I got enough money to buy you a ticket to Boston. I'm not even into my other sweat sock yet. But that wouldn't leave me any money once I got there."

"I don't want your money, Robby."

"Don't worry. You won't get it."

"Your money isn't going to last very long anyway. Hotels are expensive in big cities."

"Hey, what makes you think I'm gonna stay in a hotel? I'm staying with my pal Monk. That was his mom I was talking to on the phone when you came along. We're tight. Me and the Kellys. People in Massachusetts aren't like they are out here. They're warm and friendly. The Kellys are Catholics, and Catholics take people in. Even folks who aren't Catholics. But don't get the idea they'll take you in. 'Cause they won't. They don't even know you. Gimme the sandwich."

Suddenly I was hungry. That's what making a speech will do for you. I ate the half a sandwich. It tasted good. Even with the tomato slices. The half an apple was good too and the cookie was delicious. I was only sorry I hadn't made more sandwiches before I left. But who knew I'd run into Miss Busybody Lowenfeld? Telling me I ought to feel sorry for Dad 'cause he'd be worried about me!

I looked out the window. The farm fields were brown. Spring planting hadn't started yet. There were buds on trees. Lots of small white farmhouses surrounded by clumps of trees that acted as windbreaks. A series of low redbrick buildings came into view. I knew they were part of the state hospital. After that, there were more farms as we got farther and farther away from Arborville.

Dad worrying about me? He'd probably given up the search, taken Miss Bradsbury back to school, and was back at the house getting ready for the visit from his lady love. And Peggy was getting ready to flirt with Brian the Snot. Well, they all deserved each other. I was well out of it.

I looked at Beth. She just sat there looking straight ahead of her. She was a real pain coming along like this, but she was pretty spunky too. I had to admit that. And she'd be in a lot of trouble too. Not just at the bus station but with school and her mom. Her dad and Carol were on their honeymoon. They wouldn't even know she was gone. But her mother and her stepfather would. Mr. Harry F. Burns, big businessman.

I wondered how she got along with him.

"Hey . . ."

She looked at me. She was still sore at me. I didn't blame her. I had been a little mean with that bus station stuff, but what I had said was true.

"What?"

"What's your stepfather like?"

She shrugged. "He's all right."

"You call him Harry, don't you?"

"Yeah."

"Doesn't he want you to call him Dad?"

"No. And I wouldn't. I got a dad."

"I don't have a mom anymore, but if my dad marries your cousin or aunt or whatever she is, I wouldn't even call her Mom. Even though my mom's dead, she's still my mom. She always will be. Dad said that and Carol said it too once."

"You could call her Angela. The way I call him Harry."

Just the offhand way she said that sent a shiver through me. As though she thought it could really happen.

I hesitated a moment before asking her if she thought it really could happen. And then I did: "You think your aunt wants to marry my dad?"

Beth shrugged. "I don't know."

"Dad's an engineer. He doesn't know anything about life. He doesn't even know how to dance."

"Dancing's not important when you're married. Aunt Angela's first husband, Uncle Larry, was a great dancer and they still got divorced."

"You think she likes my dad, don't you?"

Beth nodded. "She talked a lot about him on the way home from the wedding." Beth looked at me. "I'm sorry."

"Hey, don't feel sorry for me. I'm fine. I'm getting out of this mess. Feel sorry for yourself for getting on this bus with me."

"I'm not scared," she said. "And I don't feel sorry for myself. It's just that . . . that . . ." She started to cry. It was like her mask suddenly fell off and tough little Beth Lowenfeld started to cry. "I just didn't want you to leave. I . . . like you."

Those last words were wrenched out of her.

"Beth, please stop. I like you too. A lot. You're the first girl I ever liked." I cleared my throat. I suddenly felt like crying too.

I grabbed her hand. "You know something? You're gonna like Monk Kelly and he's gonna like you too."

And that was when I realized that as soon as we got to Toledo, I was going to buy her a ticket to Boston.

There was no way I'd leave her alone in a big-city bus station.

WELCOME TO OHIO, THE BUCKEYE STATE

That sign stretched across the expressway. Our bus roared under it. So long, Michigan. At last!

The trouble was that Ohio didn't look an awful lot different. The same flat fields, the same clouds, the same sky.

After a few miles the farmland turned into subdivisions, houses, and paved streets. There were more overpasses. And on them, city buses. We passed gas stations and malls. Street signs appeared.

Under a big, green-and-white highway sign we glided off the expressway and into downtown Toledo. It was about 2:30 in the afternoon, and Toledo looked dead. There were cars going fast down wide, one-way boulevards, and sometimes you could see people in stores, but no one was out on the sidewalks. You wondered how folks got from their cars into the stores.

Lots of the buildings looked empty. One or two were boarded up. It seems to me they always put bus stations in the bad parts of cities.

I was glad Beth and I were going on together.

I wondered if Joe Dawkins and the others knew I'd taken off. Probably not. And it wouldn't make any difference to them if they did know. They didn't like me and I didn't like them.

I wondered if Dad was still with Miss Bradsbury. The only good thing to happen so far was him getting a good dose of her. He probably hadn't got a word in edgewise all afternoon.

"Toledo," the driver called out as we pulled into the parking area behind the bus station. He nosed the bus into a bay. Then, before he opened the doors, he turned in his seat and faced us.

"For them that's going on to Cleveland, there's a layover of ten minutes. We leave at 2:42 on the dot."

All the passengers rose to get off except the mother and her daughters.

"Can't we get off, Mom?" Ticia asked.

"The bus is leaving in ten minutes. We'll stay right here," the mother said in a soft voice.

"But I got to go to the bathroom," Ticia said.

Mother just looked at her and then, reluctantly, stood up.

Beth and I got off ahead of them. "OK. Let's buy you a ticket to Boston," I said.

"Couldn't we go back to Arborville together, Robby?"

After what I'd been through in my mind, I couldn't believe she'd said that. Was that what being a girl was like?

"Look, you either come with me or go back. If you

wanna go back, I'll buy you a ticket to Arborville."

She didn't say anything. But once we were inside the terminal, I saw her look around, taking it all in. She was deciding if bus stations were as bad as I said they were.

This one wasn't, really. At least not yet. There were folks around. Passengers waiting for other buses. A man mopping the floor. The bus station was well lit and clean.

But it would be a different story at night. Beth hadn't ever seen a bus station at night, filled with the homeless. People sleeping on floors. I'd seen that.

"Beth, we've only got ten minutes. Do you want a ticket to Arborville or a ticket to Boston? It's up to you."

She didn't say anything. I could tell she didn't really want to go to Boston. She'd never been there. It was a strange place. She wanted to go back home. But she wanted me to go with her, and that I couldn't do.

At least two minutes went by without her saying anything. She just looked miserable. Fortunately there was only one person at the ticket counter, so we could wait a couple more minutes. But no more than that.

"C'mon. Make up your mind."

She looked around the terminal again, and I figured she was trying to picture what it would be like to sit here alone.

"OK," I said, "you don't want to go to Boston. I'll

buy you a ticket back to Arborville. Let's find out when the next bus is due."

I got behind the man at the ticket counter. Beth didn't come with me. She didn't want to make any decision. Wouldn't she be great at shortstop deciding whether to go for a double play or get the sure out at first?

The clock on the wall said 2:37 . . . about five minutes before the 990 bus left for Cleveland. The man in front of me was asking endless questions about making a connection at Cincinnati for Louisville.

Finally, he paid for his ticket and I stepped up to the counter.

"Could you tell me when the next bus leaves for Arborville?" I asked.

The clerk glanced at a schedule. "Eight fifteen, if it's on time."

He hadn't called me 'sonny,' which already made him a lot nicer than the ticket agent in Arborville.

"The next bus to Arborville leaves at 8:15 . . . if it's on time," I called back to Beth.

That meant a layover of almost six hours.

The loudspeaker boomed out: "The 990 for Cleveland now boarding in Bay Nine. The 990 for Cleveland now boarding in Bay Nine."

"That's us, Beth. Yes or no. Do you want to come with me?"

"What time does it leave again, Robby?"

"It's leaving right now. You just heard the announcement."

"I mean the bus back to Arborville."

"I told you. Eight fifteen."

"And when does it get to Arborville?"

She was stalling, hoping I'd miss the 990.

"It takes as long as it just took us to get here. About an hour. Quit stalling."

"What does it cost?"

"You know what it costs 'cause you bought a ticket here. Listen, Beth, I know what you're doing but I'm not going to miss my bus. I'm gonna leave you enough money for a ticket and you can buy it. And I'll give you money to make a phone call to your mother."

I got out my sock with the money, and squatting down, I emptied it onto the floor of the Toledo bus station. I'm here to tell you my money hit that floor like a symphony orchestra. Everyone stopped in their tracks. Nickels, dimes, and quarters were rolling around. Beth chased some down. I swept up the quarters first.

"How much was that ticket again?" I asked her.

"I don't remember." She ran off, chasing a nickel. She was doing that on purpose so I couldn't give her the money.

The loudspeaker blared: "Last call. The 990 departing for Cleveland from Bay Nine."

I scooped up the rest of the money and put it on the ticket counter. "This is for a ticket to Arbor—"

That was as far as I got. A terrible scream split the air. I spun around.

Standing in front of the ladies room was the tall

126

mother. She had her hand over her mouth. By her side the timid twin was weeping.

The man mopping the floor threw down his mop and ran to her. So did several other people.

"What's the matter, lady?"

"What happened? What's wrong?"

The mother looked at them. She couldn't even talk. She was shaking like a leaf.

"Tell us."

"I've lost my child. She . . . she . . . went to the bathroom but she's not in there. She's not in the bus station."

And then she started to cry. It was like a huge tree going down. It was frightening.

"Did you look in the toilet?" a woman asked her. She nodded, crying.

"We'll find her, lady," the man who had been mopping said. "What's her name?"

"What's she look like?"

"Where'd you last see her?"

"What was she wearing?"

"Final call. The 990 for Cleveland leaving from Bay Nine," the speaker sounded. "All aboard."

"I'll check the ladies room again," a woman said.

"Don't you worry, lady. She's here somewhere."

I stared at the tall woman. I'd never seen anyone cry so hard in my life. You could tell she wasn't the crying kind. When strong people break down, they really break.

The timid little twin had turned her face into her

mother's dress and was bawling into it. Those little girls couldn't have been more opposite of each other. One scared to leave her mother's side. The other wanting to poke her nose into everything. And then it hit me.

"I bet I know where Ticia is," I said to Beth.

"Where?"

"C'mon!"

I ran out of the terminal. Our driver was in the bus. The door was closed. The bus was starting to back out.

"Stop!" I banged on the doors.

The bus stopped. The doors opened. "Son," the driver said, "this bus was announced three times. Get on."

"Open the luggage compartment," I yelled at him.

"What for? You can take that little bag on with you."

"It's not that. Open it!"

"You didn't put the bag in luggage before."

"Please open it."

The panic in my voice and face got to him.

"All right," he grumbled, "but I'm tellin' you, you didn't put it in there when we left Arborville."

"It's not that."

"Well, it better be something."

He turned the lever and pulled the compartment door up and Ticia came rolling out, crying.

"I'll be darned," the driver said.

14

Part of my story ends here. With Ticia weeping in her mother's arms. And the mother on her knees, holding her tight, her eyes closed.

People stood there silently watching them. The janitor, the ticket agent, passengers waiting for other buses, the Cleveland-bound passengers from 990 who got out of the bus to see what was going on, and of course, there was me and Beth and the driver.

"Kid, how'd you know she was in there?" the driver asked me.

"She wanted to see what was in there back in Arborville."

"That was good thinking," the ticket agent said. "We could've had one sick child by the time the 990 rolled into Cleveland. OK, folks, it's all over now. Any of you goin' to Cleveland better get back on. You too, ma'am. And you too, son."

I took a deep breath. "I'm not going," I said.

"What?"

"I'm going back to Arborville."

The driver looked at me and then shook his head.

"Too much. Well, I don't know where you're headed, kid, but I sure want to thank you for what you just did."

He stuck out his hand and I shook it. I think this was the first time an adult ever shook my hand to thank me for doing something.

"I want to thank you too," a soft voice said. It was the mother. Her eyes were still red.

"That's OK," I said.

"What do you say to the boy, Ticia?" the mother said. Ticia, not so wriggly anymore, was holding her mom's hand tightly.

"I'm sorry," Ticia said.

"No, Ticia, you say, 'Thank you for saving my life.' "

"Thank you for saving my life," Ticia said, and started to cry again. And this set off Timid Sister. The mother shook her head and took them to the bus.

The ticket agent, taking no chances, put them aboard personally. When the doors closed behind them, he breathed out in relief.

"Well," he said, "how about that." He looked at me. "Son, if you're going to Arborville, then maybe I better sell you a ticket there. That make sense to you?"

"Yes, sir."

"It makes sense to me too." We went into the terminal as the 990 started backing out of the bay.

"I sort of hate to charge you," the agent confided. "You're a real hero. The company ought to give you a free ride anywhere in the U.S. Of course you can

130

exchange your Cleveland ticket and get some money back."

"It's a ticket to Boston," I said.

His eyebrows shot up. "When you change your mind, I guess you really do." He took the ticket from me and examined it. "Boston, it is. Well, you have some real money coming to you now. And I take it your . . . uh . . . girl friend wants a ticket to Arborville?"

I felt my face redden. "Yes, sir," I said, not daring to look at Beth.

A bus horn blared outside. The ticket agent began punching buttons. Outside, the bus horn blared again.

Beth looked at me. "Why'd you change your mind, Robby?"

I didn't feel like telling her.

"Was it when you saw how scared her mother was? You thought about your dad?"

She was smart, all right. That was it. Though I'd never want to admit it. That mother was a strong, quiet person like Dad. I didn't want to ever picture Dad crying like that. It was too painful. Dad never cried.

The horn sounded again. A bus driver was leaning on it.

"All right, kids, here're your tickets. And you, son, get eighty-four dollars back. Usually in the case of that much refund you're supposed to fill out a form, but since you saved the company, heck, the whole city, a lot of embarrassment and bad publicity, I'm just going to give you your money right now."

The bus horn sounded again and again. The ticket agent shook his head. "It's been that kind of day, hasn't it? Well, I better go see what the matter is now."

He wasn't the only one going out to see what was going on. A lot of people were going outside.

"There's a car blocking the bus," someone said.

"Better get a cop."

Beth and I went outside, and stared.

"Oh, no," I said.

The 990 bus for Cleveland hadn't even got out of the parking lot. It was blocked at the exit by our station wagon. The Miller station wagon!

Worse yet, Dad was pounding on the door of the bus, yelling for the driver to open it up. And the bus driver, clearly thinking he had a lunatic on his hands, was blowing his horn for help.

"Warren," a voice yelled from our car, "they're not on the bus. They're over there." It was Miss Bradsbury. She was still with him.

"Robby!" Dad yelled. He ran toward me.

"Beth . . ." I whispered. "I'm scared."

I hesitated and then ran to meet Dad.

"Remind me never to drive this route again," I heard the bus driver say, as Dad and I collided and hugged and hugged and hugged oh so hard.

"Robby . . . Robby . . ."

"Dad, I'm so sorry."

"It's all right. It's over." Dad's face was wet. He was crying. I'd never seen him cry. Even after Mom died.

"Will someone get that danged car out of here? I got a schedule to keep," the bus driver shouted.

"I'll move the car, Warren," Miss Bradsbury said.

"Thank you, Janet. Where's Beth? Ah, there you are. Thank God."

The bus driver tipped his cap sarcastically to Miss Bradsbury as she moved the car. "Thanks, lady."

"All right, folks," the ticket agent said to the people gathered outside, "everything's OK. Just another ordinary day in the Toledo bus station. Tune in next hour when the bus for Cincinnati tries to leave."

Miss Bradsbury parked our car off to the side. She came over to us. "Well," she said with that faintly amused cool voice of hers. "Fancy meeting you two here." She turned to Dad. "Warren, I'm going to call Mrs. Burns and tell her we've found Beth. And Beth, you better come with me. Your mother will want to hear your voice."

She didn't say a word to me. I guess she was pretty sore at me. Dad and I were alone again.

We looked at each other. Dad took off his glasses and wiped them with his handkerchief. He always did that when he was about to say something important.

"You could have talked to me, Robby. You didn't have to run away."

I didn't answer right away. Then I said, without meeting his eyes, "You're not easy to talk to. About . . . deep stuff."

"Like Mrs. Nathanson?"

I nodded.

133

"Well, we'll talk from now on, won't we?"

"I guess."

"No, we will. We'll talk about everything. Running away's no good, Robby."

"I was coming home. That's why I wasn't on the bus."

"You changed your mind about going to Boston?"

"Yeah. And how'd you know I was going to Boston anyway?"

"I talked to the ticket agent in the Arborville bus station."

"Oh. How'd you even know I'd gone to the bus station?"

"Janet . . . Miss Bradsbury and I looked all over town for you. Finally we went back to our house. I was trying to decide whether to call the police. That was when I saw your piggy banks were missing. I don't know how I missed that the first time. Anyway, it meant one thing to me: You were buying a ticket somewhere. I called the train station and then the bus station. The ticket agent at the bus station remembered you . . ."

He would, I thought.

". . . and where you'd bought a ticket to. He also remembered selling a girl your age a ticket too. By that time we knew that Beth hadn't come back to school from lunch. Janet . . . Miss Bradsbury called Ruth Burns, and then we drove to Toledo very, very fast."

"I'm sorry, Dad."

"The important thing is we're together again. And

also . . ." Dad was looking for the right words. "Also that you changed your mind about running away. What made you stop your trip, Robby?"

I hesitated. I hadn't been able to admit it to Beth, and here was Dad asking now. I took a deep breath and told him about Ticia and how frightened her mother had been. Dad listened without saying anything. When I was done, we just looked at each other.

Then he reached over and pulled me toward him and kissed me. I kissed him back. Dad and I never kissed before. My cheeks were wet too. And not just from his.

That's what we were doing, hugging and kissing, when Miss Bradsbury and Beth came out of the terminal.

"Well," Miss Bradsbury said, observing the two of us, "things look better already."

Dad blew his nose. Then he cleared his throat. "Did you get hold of Ruth Burns?"

"We did. Both Beth and I talked to her. And you two have talked, I take it."

"We're just beginning to," Dad said.

"Hugging and kissing is a very good way to begin. Well, shall we be on our way back? I have a lot of work yet to do today," she said briskly.

She hustled us all into the car. It was like getting kids in from recess. She made Dad a schoolboy too. He didn't seem to mind.

15

It was an odd trip back. For the first few miles Miss Bradsbury talked about the foolishness of running away from home.

At one point she said that you couldn't ever really run away because you always took yourself with you.

Beth and I, seated in back, looked at each other, puzzled. She didn't get it either.

"But I think we probably ought to talk about why we ran away," Miss Bradsbury continued.

I hate that "we" teachers use when they mean "you."

"Beth?" she said, calling on Beth as though we were now in our classroom.

Beth was silent. I almost raised my hand in the backseat. I spoke up for her. "She didn't run away, Miss Bradsbury. She just tried to stop me. That's how come she was on the bus. She was still trying to talk me out of it."

Miss Bradsbury looked surprised. Dad looked at me in the rearview mirror. Didn't they know that? Did they really think Beth was running away from home too? Maybe they even thought we had planned it together. Adults are incredible.

"Is that right, Beth?" Miss Bradsbury asked.

"Yes, ma'am."

"I'd call that a real friend," Dad said softly.

"Yes, I would too," Miss Bradsbury said. And added, "Robby, would you tell Beth's mother what you just told us?"

"Sure."

"Well then, we know about Beth, but now Robby, what about you?"

She knew why I ran away. Did we have to go through this in public?

"Could my dad and I talk about it later? In private?"

"Of course you *could*. The question is will you?"

"We will," Dad said.

"Good. Then all that's left to do now is decide about making up the schoolwork you missed today. . . ."

She was really something else. She was organized, to say the least. Before we'd gone another two miles she had us agreeing that we would each call Mrs. Janssen and find out what the class had done in our absence and make it up that evening.

With all that settled, I thought maybe we'd drive in silence. But out of nowhere, Miss Bradsbury asked us if we would like to sing a round.

"A what?" I asked.

"A round. Like 'Frère Jacques' or 'Row, Row, Row Your Boat.' "

"I don't sing," I said.

"I do and I love group singing in a car. I so rarely have the opportunity to do it." Before any of us could stop her, she began singing "Frère Jacques." To my amazement Dad joined in. It was almost but not quite like those car trips in California. Mom sang different songs. Folk songs. And she didn't organize us to sing. But then, Mom wasn't a principal.

Still, there was Dad, who couldn't sing a lick, singing his fool head off.

Beth had a funny smile on her lips.

"I think they've both gone crazy," I whispered.

Smiling, she shook her head. "I don't think so," she said.

After Dad and Miss Bradsbury got done singing, they complimented each other on their great voices and then they talked about songs they remembered from their youth. They talked about songs they'd sung in summer camps. When they exhausted that topic, they talked about whether it was better to vacation in the country or by the sea. Miss Bradsbury said that in Michigan you could have both if you didn't mind your ocean being sodium free. (Salt free. A principal's joke.) It turned out that she owned a cottage in Michigan's Upper Peninsula. She told Dad how cold Lake Superior was. We had taken a vacation in Maine once, and Dad told her how cold the ocean was there. She said it couldn't be any colder than Lake Superior. Dad argued that it very well could be. Beth and I listened to them argue with each other about cold water. It was hard to believe that Dad, an engineer, a kind of scientist type, would argue about which was colder: Lake Superior or the Atlantic Ocean. In no time at all, we were back in Arborville.

We dropped Beth off first. I went to her front door with her and Miss Bradsbury. I had promised to tell Mrs. Burns why Beth had "run away."

And I did. Mrs. Burns was pretty nice about it, considering how worried she was. She had been located by a special messenger from her company and had done nothing but sit anxiously by the telephone. She politely thanked me for explaining all that and she thanked Miss Bradsbury for personally looking for Beth. She also waved at Dad, who had stayed in our station wagon. I knew they'd talk about it together later.

I also knew that Beth was going to catch it privately later. Just like Ticia the Wriggly probably would.

Miss Bradsbury and I headed back to the car.

"Thank you, Robby," she said quietly. "You were very forthright."

I wasn't sure what "forthright" meant, but it sounded OK.

"Beth Lowenfeld is a very nice person, isn't she?" she said.

I nodded.

"I hope you'll be very nice to her for a long time to come."

God, that annoyed me. Telling me to be nice to someone I liked a lot already. Couldn't principals every stop "principaling"?

"How did it go?" Dad asked.

"Mrs. Burns is upset, of course, but Robby told her it was his fault. I can only hope she believes him and won't be too hard on Beth. I think things will be all right there. And now, Mr. Miller, if you'll kindly take me back to school . . ."

She had been calling him "Warren." Suddenly it was Mr. Miller again. I didn't get it.

"Isn't school over, Miss Bradsbury? I see kids coming home."

And he was calling her "Miss Bradsbury." What were they up to?

"School is over for the pupils, Mr. Miller, but not for the teachers, and most certainly not for the principal, especially not for this principal who took the afternoon off."

I blushed. She laughed. So did Dad.

"Janet," Dad said suddenly, "what are you doing for supper tonight?"

She was surprised. "Supper? Well, I haven't given it much thought."

"Could I talk you into having supper with us tonight? Peggy is home thawing out the casseroles and, as you know . . ." Dad paused. He glanced back over his shoulder at me. "I guess you don't know this, Robby."

"Don't know what?"

"Before we set out for the bus station, I called Mrs. Nathanson and told her we'd have to take a rain check on tonight. At that time I didn't know how far we'd have to drive to catch up with your bus."

"We *were* prepared to go as far as Boston," Miss Bradsbury said.

Dad laughed. "Albany, Janet, Albany. Anyway, Peg doesn't know a thing about this. She still thinks Mrs. Nathanson and Brian are coming. Janet, will you join us for supper?"

"I'd be happy to, provided you drive me home right now so I can pick up dessert."

"You're going to make a dessert now?"

"No." She laughed. "But being a working woman who loves to cook and eat, I made and froze some pies over the weekend. So, Warren, I accept your kind invitation on the condition you let me unfreeze a pie . . . in my office."

"Your proviso is accepted. Where do you live?"

"Off Pauline Boulevard. Do you know where that is?"

Dad shook his head.

"It's the west side."

"I don't think I've ever been on the west side of Arborville."

"Shame on you. You've probably traveled all over the country and the world and haven't yet seen the west side of the town you live in?"

"I guess that's right," Dad said apologetically.

"I think that's dreadful. And we shall certainly correct that immediately. Turn right on Packard."

"And then?"

"Left on Hoover. And after that a new world will open up for you."

141

Dad laughed. So did she. I could have been in China as far as they were concerned. Or Boston.

We went into her house to get her pie. It was a neat little house with books all over. After that, we drove back to school. Kids were playing in front of the school. Among them, kids from our team. I spotted Joe Dawkins and ducked.

Dad and I drove home. He didn't get out of the car.

"I've got a few things to attend to at the office, Robby. I'll be home within a half hour. Will you please let Peggy know about the changes?"

"She's going to be sore."

"I expect she will. And you better call Mrs. Janssen and find out what work you missed. Janet will be checking up on you later this evening."

"Why do you call her Janet?"

"Because that's her name." He drove away.

I was fishing for my house key when our front door opened, and there stood Peg in the red-flowered apron that had belonged to Mom.

"What's going on, Robby?"

"What do you mean?"

"The phone's been ringing ever since I got home from school. And your friends have been coming over."

"What friends?"

"Joe Dawkins and Littlefield."

"They're not my friends."

"Well, they think they are. They said to tell you they're playing ball in front of the school."

"I saw them." I brushed by her.

"What did you do today, anyway?" she called after me.

"Nothing." I went into the kitchen and got out a Pepsi.

The kitchen was all cleaned up. The casseroles were out of the freezer and ready to be put into the oven. I suddenly felt sorry for Peg.

"Why did they keep wanting to know if you were back yet? Did you go somewhere?"

"To Toledo." The whole house was probably spotless. I felt awful for her.

"Toledo. Very funny. How about going upstairs and showering, and changing your shirt and pants. Do you have cleaner sneakers?"

"No."

"Then wear shoes."

"Peg . . ." It wasn't going to be easy to break the news to her. She had every right to hit me over the head with a frying pan.

"Brian and his mother will be dressed, Robby. So will Dad. I'm going to change too."

I stared at my Pepsi. "They're not coming, Peg."

"What?"

"They're not coming."

"What do you mean they're not coming?"

I noticed the red light was on on the stove. She was preheating it for the casseroles.

She stepped around me and stood between me and the stove. "What do you mean they're not coming?"

"Dad called them up and canceled it."

143

"That's crazy. Why would he do that? He would have called me if he'd done that."

"He didn't have time to call you, Peg. He . . . he was out of town too."

Without thinking, she turned off the stove. I turned it back on. "Someone else is coming."

She stared at me. "What's going on, Robby?" Her voice was scared a little.

"It's a long story. I'm sorry. It's all my fault. But . . . uh . . . Miss Bradsbury is coming for dinner."

Peg almost fell over. "Your principal?"

"Yeah. Dad invited her."

"I don't understand. I don't understand what's happening."

"I don't either." Which was partly true. I didn't understand either why Miss Bradsbury had to come to dinner.

"Anyway, she's coming and she's bringing a pie for dessert."

"Where's Dad?"

"He's at his office."

"I'm going to call him and find out just what is going on."

"He's pretty busy, Peg. He'll be home soon. I can explain a lot of it. But—"

I was saved by the bell. The doorbell. I practically sprinted out of the kitchen. Peg followed me.

At the front door were Joe Dawkins and Littlefield. They had gloves, a bat, a ball.

"Raspberry told us you'd come back home," Joe said, looking awkward.

"You wanna hit a ball around with us?" Littlefield asked.

"No." I started to close the door. Peg held it open with her foot.

"Come back home from where? I want to know just what's going on."

"I told you before. From Toledo."

"You were serious?"

"Yeah."

"What were you doing in Toledo?"

"He and Beth Lowenfeld ran away together," Littlefield said, like the jerk he was.

"Beth didn't run away," I said. "I did."

"I don't believe this," Peggy said.

"All the other teams have started practicing, Robby," Joe said. "Coach won't mind if we start without her. We'd . . . uh . . . like you to play with us." He was embarrassed. "We found out from Mrs. Janssen why you . . . picked those fights. We want to apologize for not knowing those awful people were coming to your house today."

"What awful people?" Peggy asked.

I didn't dare look at Peg.

"Anyway," Joe went on, "how about playing some ball with us?"

"I can't, Joe. We got company for supper tonight."

Joe didn't say anything for a second. Then he stuck out his hand. "Friends?" he asked.

I hesitated and then I said: "Sure." And I shook hands with Joe and then I shook hands with Littlefield and then they left. And now I had to face Peg.

145

"All right, little brother. Start from the beginning. What did you do today?"

I told her. I told her everything. And when I was done, she was dazed. Anger would come later. I'd wrecked all her plans again.

"I'm sorry, Peg. I'll try to make it up to you . . . somehow."

Before she could recover enough to be sore at me, I ran upstairs and made two phone calls. The first was to Mrs. Janssen, who spoke to me as though nothing had happened. As though I'd missed school because I had a cold. She gave me the reading assignments. The other phone call went to Watertown.

An old familiar voice answered.

"Hello."

"Monk, it's me . . . Robby."

"Hey, man, where are ya?"

"In Arborville."

"In Abahville? What're ya doin' there?"

"Listen, I can't come. But maybe this summer . . ."

"But my mom said you was callin' from the bus station."

"I was. But I changed my mind. Listen, I'll write you a letter. It's a mess. Monk, I was runnin' away from home. But . . . I came back."

Silence. And then I heard Monk yell: "It's Robby. He was runnin' away from home. But he went back. He ain't comin'."

I heard his mother say something. And then Monk said: "OK." And into the phone to me, he said: "My

146

ma says she thought maybe you were doing that. You OK, man?"

"I am now. Tell your mom I'm sorry." And then I had to change the subject. "How's the team doin'?"

"Hey, we had our first practice this afternoon. And we got no shortstop."

I laughed. "We got two of them."

"Two? The other guy as good as you?"

"It's a girl. And I'll let you know."

"Yeah. And I wanna know about the runnin' away from home. Man, that's serious stuff."

"I'll write you all about it. It's a long story."

"Don't make it too long, man. You know I ain't much of a reader. Keep it short and simple."

I laughed. "I'll try, Monk."

16

Well, I tried to keep my story short and simple, but it wasn't easy to do. Things that happen to kids aren't always short or simple.

Even Miss Bradsbury coming over that night with her thawed apple pie. That should have been short and simple, but it wasn't. We had warmed-up casserole and warmed-up apple pie, but when the evening was over and Dad was seeing her to her car, I also had a warmed-up Peg. She had recovered and she was sore. "Do you see what you've done, you idiot?"

"I ran away. It was dumb. I'm sorry."

"You ran away and brought Dad and her together."

"What're you talking about?"

"I'm talking about *Janet* and *Warren*," she said, mimicking the way Dad and Miss Bradsbury talked. "Can't you see what's happening? Can't you hear it? Are you that thick?"

I guess I was that thick.

"Dad likes her. She likes him. Do you really want your principal to be your stepmother?"

"No."

I didn't. It'd be the last thing in the world I'd want. We'd be singing rounds at home, going over homework, school would never end. It would be awful.

When I told Beth a couple of days later what Peg had said, she smiled a knowing little smile.

"Don't tell me you agree with her?"

"When we were driving back from Toledo, Robby, I thought they were kind of . . ." She grinned. "Falling in love?"

Maybe girls have antennae out for that kind of thing. But maybe those antennae don't always pick up the right signals. Lots of people call each other by their first names and don't get married. I guess time would tell. Time could take care of a lot of problems.

For instance, time took care of Peg being sore at me. Two things happened. One, we found out from Carol that by the terms of her divorce, Mrs. Nathanson had to get her ex-husband's permission to move out of state with Brian, and he would not give it. So she decided to stay in California. It just wouldn't have worked out with Dad and Mrs. Nathanson.

Not unless we moved back to California, and Peggy wouldn't want to do that. Which brings up reason number two why Peg's no longer sore at me. When school started in September, she discovered a boy named Dale in her art class. I guess he's "cute" and likes her too. Brian's history.

Unfortunately, Miss Bradsbury isn't . . . yet. It's been six months since she and Dad got to know each other

149

on the way to Toledo . . . and back. Now they go together to concerts and movies and she eats at our
house and we eat at hers and I have to admit she
makes great pies. We don't sing rounds (that must
have been a one-time shot to cover awkward mo-
ments) and she doesn't ask me if I've done my homework. She's really not so bad, and when we bump
into each other in the halls at school, she says "Hello,
Robby," in the same tone of voice she uses to every
kid in the school. She's cool.

Maybe she and Dad will get married. I've stopped
thinking about it. There's nothing I could or should
do about it anyway. I learned that lesson. But if they
do marry, I hope it's when I'm in junior high.

I still don't think Miss Bradsbury is as nice as
Carol, but Carol's married, and besides, she's our
coach and it would be tricky, I think, having your
stepmother as coach. Which, of course, is what Beth
has. And I have to admit they both handle it pretty
well. Beth has come to like Carol a lot, as I always
knew she would. And Carol always liked Beth.

Carol turned out to be a good coach. We ended up
8 and 3 on the season. Pretty good, considering they
were 2 and 9 last year.

Carol didn't take any guff off the man coaches we
played against. And she ran great practices. Right
from the start. She knew what she wanted to get from
each practice. Fielding, batting, fundamentals in base
running, throwing—hitting the cut-off man—that kind
of stuff. She was tough but she was always fair. And
she knew how to handle every kid on the team.

When she got back from her honeymoon it took her only one practice to decide who was going to start at shortstop: me or Beth. Carol said we were both equally good at short but I made the pivot at second better. Therefore Beth would start at short-stop.

Smart, wasn't she?

I thought Beth would be happy with Carol's decision, but she's so tough. She wanted to have her cake and eat it too.

"I don't think you make the pivot better than me," she said when we were walking home after that first practice.

"I don't either."

Beth frowned. She didn't like me agreeing with her that fast.

"Are you sayin' Carol picked me because . . ."

"She's your stepmother?"

"Is that what you think?"

"Nope. I think she was letting me down easy. She really thinks you're a better shortstop than I am."

"What do you think?"

"I'd like to see how you do in game situations."

She snapped a bubble off. "You will." Then she looked at me. "Do you think our team could beat your old Watertown team?"

I could tell the answer was important to her. I thought about it a moment.

"Yeah. I think we could. But not if you and I were playing for them. Which," I said with a laugh, "we could be right now if it wasn't for Ticia the Wriggly."

Beth was startled. And then she laughed too. And there we were laughing about stuff that had been awful just a week before.

My story ends here. I don't know if I'm any smarter now than before, but between Carol's wedding and my running away, I've learned a couple of things. One, that life isn't always like baseball. Sometimes you just have to sit back and let the ground balls play you. In other words, you can't control everything and life won't end if you do get hit in the Adam's apple once in a while.

Secondly, I learned that you don't know till something bad happens to you who your friends are. A friend is someone who'll be there for you no matter how tough things get. A friend is there when you need him . . . or her. That's what it means to be a friend.

Oh, I'm lucky to have a father like Dad, a sister like Peg, a principal like Miss Bradsbury. I'm also very lucky to have a friend like Beth.

Even if she turned out to be a better shortstop than me. Which she did.

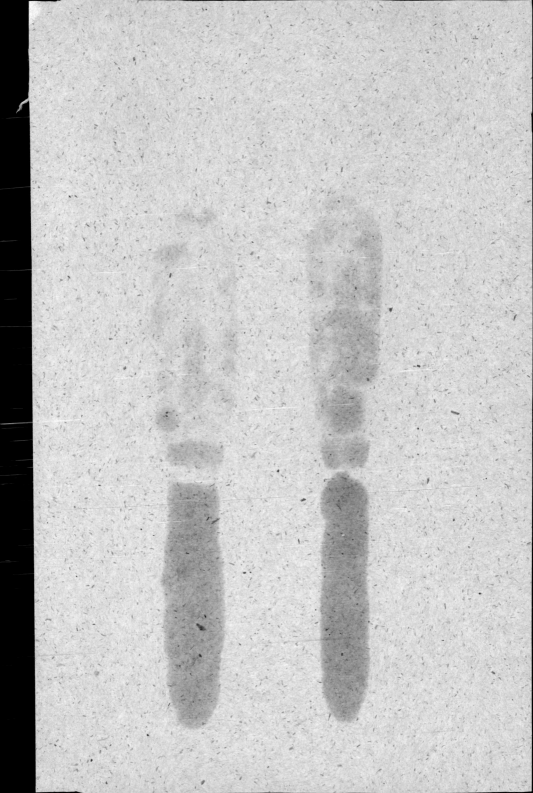